Frederick Swartwout Cozzens

The Sayings of Dr. Bushwhacker and other Learned Men

Frederick Swartwout Cozzens

The Sayings of Dr. Bushwhacker and other Learned Men

ISBN/EAN: 9783743382657

Manufactured in Europe, USA, Canada, Australia, Japa

Cover: Foto ©Andreas Hilbeck / pixelio.de

Manufactured and distributed by brebook publishing software (www.brebook.com)

Frederick Swartwout Cozzens

The Sayings of Dr. Bushwhacker and other Learned Men

AGATHYNIAN PRESS.

TO

HON. GULIAN C. VERPLANCK,

FIRST PRESIDENT

OF THE

Century Club,

THIS VOLUME

IS RESPECTFULLY DEDICATED.

PREFACE.

I HAVE dedicated this little volume of essays to Mr. Verplanck, not only because of his constant and kindly feelings, always expressed toward the Editor; not only because of the constant and kindly interest he has taken in the literary efforts of all younger American authors; nor yet from mere admiration of his vast acquirements in all fields of knowledge; nor from his extensive life-long labors for the public welfare, during which patriotism and disinterestedness, far-reaching wisdom and patient modesty, have been his constant companions; nor yet because he is one of the few left of the illustrious literary past; nor yet from the long tradition of his pure and spotless life, as befits the Christian gentleman; nor from any, or all of these, but simply because I felt that some affectionate tribute was due from me to him—my honored and venerable friend.

The papers included in this volume are partly from the *Wine Press*, a monthly periodical, which I edited for seven years—until the breaking out of the civil war—with some new articles, and with various essays of the author, that have heretofore been printed on the sands of fugitive magazines and newspapers. Some of these shells and pebbles I have reclaimed ; the rest lie upon the beach unnoticed, and, happily, unknown.

From the original articles contibuted to the *Wine Press*—independent of the author's own— I have selected some others to grace this little book. The articles, " Was Champagne known to the Ancients," and " Oxyporian Wines," are from the pen of Mr. Verplanck ; Mr. Paul Dinet, of Ay, Champagne, wrote " A French Breakfast," a composition of his own, but which, with an au- thor's license, he attributed to Brillat Savarin. Professor Walcott Gibbs, who has as exquisite a taste for true humor as any writer in the country, translated the " Hare and the Hedgehog," a story that will commend itself whenever you read it to the little people; aye, and sometimes to older folks, as I have experiencd. Mr. Chas. G. Leland, wrote the "Dainty Hints," to Epicurean Smokers; Mr. Henry P. Leland contributed the sparkling sketch of "A German Wine Cellar;" and Col. Peter A. Porter, who lost his life at the battle of Cold Harbor, in leading a charge at the head of his gallant regiment (the 8th New York Artillery), contributed the excellent imitation of Macauley's History of England. Those who knew him best will appreciate how much the Empire State has lost in losing him. The article "Does Queen Victoria Speak English," and "Sitka," were written originally for the *New York Ledger*. By the courtesy of Mr. Bonner, I have included them in this volume.

To General Wm. A. Hammond, late Surgeon General of the United States Army, I owe my thanks for his indefatigable perseverance in urging me to collect these papers. If they find any success with the public, thanks be to him who urged me to publish them, and took the greater task in preparing them for the press.

CHESTNUT COTTAGE, July 20th, 1867.

CONTENTS.

THE SAYINGS OF DR. BUSHWHACKER,

AND OTHER LEARNED MEN.

I.

A Talk About Tea.

"SIR," said our learned friend, Dr. Bushwhacker, "we are indebted to China for the four principal blessings we enjoy. Tea came from China, the compass came from China, printing came from China, and gunpowder came from China—thank God! China, sir, is an old country, a very old country. There is one word, sir, we got from China, that is oftener in the mouths of American people than any other word in the language. It is *cash*, sir, cash! That we derive from the Chinese. It is the name, sir, of the small brass coin they use, the coin with a square hole in the middle. And then look at our Franklin; he drew the lightning from

1

the skies with his kite : but who invented the kite, sir ?
The long-tailed Chinaman, sir. Franklin had no invention : he never would have invented a kite or a printing-
press. But he could use them, sir, to the best possible
advantage, sir; he had no genius, sir, but he had remarkable talent and industry. Then, sir, we get our umbrella
from China; the first man that carried an umbrella, in
London, in Queen Anne's reign, was followed by a mob.
That is only one hundred and fifty years ago. We get
the art of making porcelain from China. Our ladies must
thank the Celestials for their tea-pots. Queen Elizabeth
never saw a tea-pot in her life. In 1664, the East India
Company bought two pounds two ounces of tea as a present for his majesty, King Charles the Second. In 1667,
they imported one hundred pounds of tea. Then, sir,
rose the reign of scandal—Queen Scandal, sir! Then,
sir, rose the intolerable race of waspish spinsters who
sting reputations and defame humanity over their dys-
peptic cups. Then, sir, the astringent principle of the
herb was communicated to the heart, and domestic troubles
were brewed and fomented over the tea-table. Then, sir,
the age of chivalry was over, and women grew acrid and
bitter; then, sir, the first temperance society was founded,
and high duties were laid upon wines, and in consequence
they distilled whiskey instead, which made matters a great
deal better, of course ; and all the abominations, all the
difficulties of domestic life, all the curses of living in a
country village ; the intolerant canvassing of character.

reputation, piety: the nasty, mean, prying spirit; the uncharitable, defamatory, gossiping, tale bearing, whispering, unwomanly, unchristianlike behavior of those who set themselves up for patterns over their vile decoctions, sir, arose with the introduction of tea. Yes, sir; when the wine-cup gave place to the tea-cup, then the devil, sir, reached his culminating point. The curiosity of Eve was bad enough: but, sir, when Eve's curiosity becomes sharpened by turgid tonics, and scandal is added to inquisitiveness, and innuendo supplies the place of truth, and an imperfect digestion is the pilot instead of charity: then, sir, we must expect to see human nature vilified, and levity condemned, and good fellowship condemned, and all good men, from Washington down, damned by Miss Tittle, and Miss Tattle, and the Widow Blackleg, and the whole host of tea-drinking conspirators against social enjoyment." Here Dr. Bushwhacker grew purple with eloquence and indignation. We ventured to remark that he had spoken of tea "as a blessing" at first. "Yes, sir," responded Dr. Bushwhacker, shaking his bushy head, "that reminds one of Doctor Pangloss. Yes, sir, it is a blessing, but like all other blessings it must be used *temperately*, or else it is a curse! China, sir," continued the Doctor, dropping the oratorical, and taking up the historical. "China, sir, knows nothing of perspective, but she is great in pigments. Indian ink, sir, is Chinese, so are vermillion and indigo: the malleable properties of gold, sir, were first discovered by this extraordinary people; we must thank them for our gold leaf. Gold is not a pigment, but roast pig is, and Charles Lamb says the origin of roast pig is Chinese; the beautiful fabric we call silk, sir, came from the Flowery Nation, so did embroidery, so did the game of chess, so did fans. In fact, sir, it is difficult to say what we have not derived from the Chinese. Cotton, sir, is our great staple, but they wove and spun long staple and short staple, yellow cotton and white cotton before Columbus sailed out of the port of Palos in the Santa Maria."

"But, Doctor, we want a word with you about tea. A little information, if you please."

The Doctor is one of our old Knickerbockers. His big, bushy head is as familiar as the City Hall. He belongs to the "God bless you my dear young friend" school! He is as full of knowledge as an egg is full of meat. He knows more about China than the Emperor of the celestial people.

"Tea, my young friend, is a plant that grows in China, Japan, and other parts of the world. There are two varieties. *Thea nigra* and *Thea viridis*—black tea and green tea. The same plant, sir, produces both kinds. Green tea is made by one kind of manipulation, black tea by another. That is all, sir. The shrub is raised from seeds like hazel nuts, planted in nurseries; it is set out when about a foot high; lives for fifteen or twenty years, grows sometimes as tall as General Scott and

sometimes as small as Bill Seward. It is picked four
times a year. The first picking is the best, when the
leaves are covered with a whitish down. This is in April,
the next is in May, the next in July, the last in August.
One Chinaman can pick about thirteen pounds of leaves
per day, for which he will receive sixty *cash*, or six cents.
The green leaves are spread out on bamboo frames to dry
a little, the yellow and old defective leaves are picked out,
then they take up a handful of the leaves, cast them in a
heated pan, get them warmed up, and squeeze out the
superfluous juice; this juice contains an acrid oil, so acrid
as to irritate the hands of the workman. Good God!
think of that, sir, what stuff for the stomach. Then they
dry them slightly in the sun, then every separate leaf is
rolled up into a little ball like a shot, then they throw these
green tea shot into a pan slightly heated, stirring them
up so as to warm every part alike; then they cool the
tea, and the shot are picked out one by one, the best for
the first or finest chop. Every little ball picked over by
hand. Then it is packed, sir. The young leaves make
the ' Young Hyson,' the older and stronger leaves the
' Hyson,' the refuse goes by the name of ' Hyson Skin,'
the 'Gunpowder' and 'Imperial' are teas rolled more carefully in rounder balls than the others. Most of these teas
are colored for our market—colored, sir, with a mixture
of Prussian blue and gypsum; no wonder John Chinaman calls us outside barbarians, when he knows we drink
half a pound of gypsum and Prussian blue with every

hundred pounds of green tea, and this tea is made to order! Does honest John ever drink such tea? No, sir, he knows better than that if he does wear a tail."

"And black tea, you say, is from the same plant, Doctor?"

"Yes, sir, Mr. Robert Fortune brought specimens of the *Thea nigra* from the Bohea mountains and compared them with the *Thea viridis*, and the plants were identical. The black tea, sir, is prepared in a different manner from the other. The leaves are allowed to lie spread out on the bamboo trays for a considerable time; then they are thrown up into the air by the workman, tossed about, beat, patted, until they become soft or flaccid, then tossed in heaps, allowed to lie until they begin to change color, then they are tossed in a tea-pan, roasted over a hotter fire, rolled, shaken out, exposed to the air again, turned over, partially dried, put in the pan a second time for five minutes or so, then rolled, tossed over, and tumbled again, then put into a sieve, put over the fire again, rolled about, put over again, three or four times, then placed in a basket, thickly packed together; the Chinaman makes a hole through the mass of leaves with his hand to give vent to the smoke and steam; then over the fire they go, and remain there until they are perfectly dry—in fact, sir, until the fire dies out. Then picked, packed, and assorted for the market. Now, sir, here is the difference between black tea and green tea, the latter retains all its acrid properties, it produces nervous irritability, sleeplessness, sir; why, if you take a pinch of green tea and chew it, sir, you can sit and listen to Dr. ———'s sermon and keep wide awake sir—a thing impossible to do under any other circumstances. But black tea has much of this oil dried out of it, and therefore it is less injurious than the other; less injurious, I say, not harmless by any means. Do you ever travel in the country? Well, sir, there you will see the ravages of green tea, Prussian blue, and gypsum among the fairest portion of creation— women! There, sir, you will see pinched-up, penurious, prying faces—faces made up of a complication of fine lines, as if all human sympathies had got into a tangle; necks all wrinkles; fingers, a beautiful exhibition of bones, ligaments, and tendons; eyes, sharp, restless, inquisitive; shoulders, drooping; bust, nowhere; viscera, collapsed, and the muscular system, or the form divine generally, in a state of dubiety; yes, sir, and all this comes from the constant use of ' *Thea viridis*,' sir, green tea, sir. Our forefathers, sir, threw the tea overboard in Boston harbor; if people knew what we of the faculty know, sir, they would do the same thing now, sir, with every chop that comes from the celestial empire."

II

Journey around a Tapioca Pudding.

Dr. Bushwhacker folded his napkin, drew it through the silver ring, laid it on the table, folded his arms, leaned back in his chair, by which we knew there was something at work in his knowledge-box. "My dear Madam," said he, with a Metamora shake of the head, "there are a great many things to be said about that pudding."

Now, such a remark at a season of the year when eggs are five for a shilling, and not always fresh at that, is enough to discomfort any body. The Doctor perceived it at once, and instantly added, "In a *geographical* point of view, there are many things to be said about that pudding. My dear madam," he continued, "take tapioca itself; what is it, and where does it come from?"

Our eldest boy, just emerging from chickenhood, answered, "85 Chambers street, two doors below the Irving House."

"True, my dear young friend," responded the Doctor, with a friendly pat on the head; "true, but that is not what I mean. Where," he repeated, with a questioning look through his spectacles, and a Bushwhackian nod, "does tapioca come from?"

8

"Rio de Janeiro and Pará!"

"Yes, sir; from Rio de Janeiro in the southern, and Pará in the northern part of the Brazils, do we get our tapioca; from the roots of a plant called the Mandioca, botanically, the *Jatropha Manihot*, or, as they say, the Cassava. The roots are long and round, like a sweet potato; generally a foot or more in length. Every joint of the plant will produce its roots like the cuttings of a grape-vine. The tubers are dug up from the ground, peeled, scraped, or grated, then put in long sacks of flexible rattan; sacks, six feet long or more, and at the bottom of the sack they suspend a large stone, by which the flexible sides are contracted, and then out pours the cassava-juice in a pan placed below to receive it. This juice is poisonous, sir, highly poisonous, and very volatile. Then, my dear madam, it is macerated in water, and the residuum, after the volatile part, the poison, is evaporated, is the innocuous farina, which looks like small crumbs of bread, and which we call tapioca. The best kind of tapioca comes from Rio, which is, I believe, about five thousand five hundred miles from New York; so we must put down that as a little more than one fifth of our voyage around the pudding."

This made our eldest open his eyes.

"Eggs and milk," continued Dr. Bushwhacker, "are home productions; but sugar, refined sugar, is made partly of the moist and sweet yellow sugar of Louisiana, partly of the hard and dry sugar of the West Indies; I will not go into the process of refining sugar now, but I may observe here, that the sugar we get from Louisiana, if refined and made into a loaf, would be quite soft, with large loose crystals, while the Havana sugar, subjected to the same treatment, would make a white cone almost as compact and hard as granite. But we have made a trip to the Antilles for our sugar, and so you may add fifteen hundred miles more for the saccharine."

"That is equal to nearly one-third of the circumference of the pudding we live upon, Doctor."

"Vanilla," continued the Doctor, "with which this pudding is so delightfully flavored, is the bean of a vine that grows wild in the multitudinous forests of Venezuela, New Granada, Guiana, and, in fact, throughout South America. The long pod, which looks like the scabbard of a sword, suggested the name to the Spaniards; vagna, meaning scabbard, from which comes the diminutive, vanilla, or little scabbard—appropriate enough, as every one will allow. These beans, which are worth here from six to twenty dollars a pound, could be as easily cultivated as hops in that climate; but the indolence of the people is so great, that not one Venezuelian has been found with sufficient enterprise to set out one acre of vanilla, which would yield him a small fortune every year. No, sir. The poor peons, or peasants, raise their garabanzas for daily use, but beyond that they never look. They plant their crops in the footsteps of their ancestors, and, if it had not been for their ancestors, they would probably have browsed on the wild grass of the llanos or plains. Ah! there are a great many such bobs hanging at the tail of some ancestral kite, even in this great city, my dear, learned friend."

"True, Doctor, you are right there."

"Well, sir, the vanilla is gathered from the wild vines in the woods. Off goes the hidalgo, proud of his noble ancestry, and toils home under a back-load of the refuse beans from the trees, after the red monkey has had his pick of the best. A few reals pay him for the day's work, and then, hey for the cock-pit! There, Signor Olfogie meets the Marquis de Shinplaster, or the Padre Corcorochi, and of course gets whistled out of his earnings with the first click of the gaffs. Then back he goes to his miserable hammock, and so ends his year's labor. That, sir, is the history of the flavoring, and you will have to allow a stretch across the Caribbean, say twenty-five hundred miles, for the vanilla."

"We are getting pretty well around, Doctor."

"Then we have sauce, here, wine-sauce; Teneriffe, I should say, by the flavor.

'—— from beneath the cliff
Of sunny-sided Teneriffe,
And ripened in the blink
Of India's sun.'

We must take four thousand miles at least for the wine, my learned friend, and say nothing of the rest of the sauce."

"Except the nutmeg, Doctor."

"Thank you, my dear young friend, thank you. The nutmeg! To the Spice Islands, in the Indian Ocean we are indebted for our nutmegs. Our old original Knickerbockers, the web-footed Dutchmen, have the monopoly of this trade. Every nutmeg has paid toll at the Hague before it yields its aroma to our graters. The Spice Islands! The almost fabulous Moluccas, where neither corn nor rice will grow; where the only quadrupeds they have are the odorous goats that breathe the fragrant air, and the musky crocodiles that bathe in the high-seasoned waters. The Moluccas,

> '—— the isles
> Of Ternate and Tidore, whence merchants bring
> Their spicy drugs.'

There, sir! Milton, sir. From Ternate and Tidore, and the rest of that marvellous cluster of islands, we get our nutmegs, our mace, and our cloves. Add twelve thousand miles at least to the circumference of the pudding for the nutmeg."

"This is getting to be a pretty large pudding, Doctor."

"Yes, sir. We have traveled already twenty-five thousand five hundred miles around it, and now let us re-circumnavigate and come back by the way of Mexico, so that we can get a silver spoon, and penetrate into the interior."

III.

The Radiant Dinner=Castor.

WE begin to think there is wisdom in Dr. Bush-whacker. "There are other things to study geography from, besides maps and globes," is one of his favorite maxims. We begin to believe it. "Observe my learned friend," said he, "how the reflected sunshine from those cut bottles in the castor-stand, throws long plumes of light in every direction across the white damask." We leaned forward, and saw the phenomenon pointed out by the index-finger of the Doctor, and as we knew something was coming from his pericranics, kept silent of course. "Well," said he, inflating his lips until his face looked like that of a cast-iron caryatid, "well, my dear friend, every pencil of light there is a point of the compass, and the contents of that castor come from places as various as those diverging rays indicate. The mustard is from England, the vinegar from France, China furnishes the soy, Italy the oil, we have to ask the West Indies to contribute the red-pepper, and the East Indies to supply the black-pepper." We ventured to remark that those facts we were not ignorant of, by any means. "True, my dear learned friend," said the Doctor, with a sort of snort; "but God bless me! if one-half of the

13

people in this city know it." "Mustard," continued
Doctor Bushwhacker, not at all discomfited, "comes
from Durham, in the north of England—that is, the best
quality. The other productions of this county do not
amount to much, nor is it celebrated for any thing,
except that here the Queen Philippa, wife of King
Edward the Third, captured David Bruce, King of Scots,
for which reason no Scotchman can eat Durham mustard
except with tears in his eyes. We get our grindstones
from this English county, my learned friend; and when
you sharpen your knife or your appetite hereafter, it will
remind you of Durham. That long pencil of light from
the next bottle points to France, where they make the
best wine-vinegar we get. Just observe the difference
between that sturdy, pot-bellied mustard-bottle, which
represents John Bull, and this slender sharp, vinegar-
cruet, which represents Johnny Crapeau; there is a
national distinction sir, in cruets as well as men. The
quantity of vinegar made in France is very great, the
best comes from Bordeaux; sometimes it is so strong that
the Frenchmen call it '*vinaigre des trois dents*,' or vinegar with three teeth; but the finest flavored vinegar I
ever met with came from Portugal, and for a salad, nothing could equal its delicate aroma. Well, sir, then there
is the red-pepper, the Cayenne; that I presume is from
Jamaica?" We assented.

"The best and strongest kind is made partly of the bird
pepper, and partly of the long-pod pepper of the West

Indies. This is a very healthy condiment, sir; in the tropics it is indispensable; there is a maxim there, sir, that people who eat Cayenne pepper will live for ever. Like variety, it is the spice of life, sir, at the equator. Our own gardens, sir, furnish capsicum, and in fact it grows in all parts of the world; but that from the West Indies is esteemed to be the best, and I think with justice. Now, sir, the next pencil of light is reflected from the Yellow Sea!"

"The soy, Doctor?"

"The soy, my learned friend; the best fish-sauce on the face of the globe. The soy, sir, or 'soya,' as the Japanese call it, is a species of bean, which would grow in this country as well as any other Chinese plant. Few Chinamen eat anything without a mixture of this bean-jelly in some shape or other. They scald and peel the beans, then add an equal quantity of wheat or barley, then the mess is allowed to ferment, then they add a little salt, sometimes tumeric for color, water is added also, in the proportion of three to one of the mass, and after a few months' repose the soy is pressed, strained, and ready for market. That, sir, is the history of that cruet, and now we will pass on to the black pepper."

"A glass of wine first, Doctor, if you please."

"Thank you, my dear friend; bless me, how dry I am."

"Black pepper, *piper nigrum*, is the berry of a vine that grows in Sumatra and Ceylon, but our principal supply of this commonest of condiments comes from the Island of Java; and we have to pay our web-footed Knickerbockers, across the water, a little toll upon that, as we do upon many other things of daily consumption. The pepper-vine is a very beautiful plant, with large, oval, polished leaves and showy white flowers, that would look beautiful if wound around the head of a bride."

"No doubt, Doctor, but I think the less pepper about a bride the better."

"Good, my learned friend; you are right; if I were to get married again, sir," continued the Doctor in a very hearty manner, "I should be a little afraid of the contact of *piper nigrum.*"

"What is white pepper, Doctor?"

"White pepper is the same, sir, as black pepper, only it is decorticated, that is, the black husk has been rubbed off. Now, sir, there is not much else interesting about pepper, except that the best probably comes from the kingdom of Bantam; and the quantity, formerly export-ed from the seaport of that name in the Island of Java, amounted, sir, to ten thousand tons annually; a good seasonable supply of seasoning for the world, sir. Well, sir, we are also indebted to Bantam for a very small breed of fowls, the peculiar use of which no philosopher has as yet been able to determine. Now, sir, we have finished the castor, I think?"

"There is one point of light, Doctor, that indicates Italy; what of the oil?"

"Ah! Lucca and Parma! Indeed, sir, I may say, France, Spain, and Italy!

'Three kingdoms claim its birth;
Both hemispheres proclaim its worth.'

The olive, sir. I remember something from my school-boy days about that. It is from Pliny's History of Nature, sir. (Liber. XV.) The olive in the western world was the companion, sir, as well as the symbol of peace. Two centuries after the foundation of Rome, both Italy and Africa were strangers to this useful plant. It was naturalized in those countries, sir, and at length carried into the heart of Spain and Gaul. The timid errors of the ancients, that it required a certain degree of heat, and could not flourish in the neighborhood of the sea, were insensibly exploded by industry and experience. There, sir! But the timid errors of the ancients are not more surprising than the timid errors of the moderns. The olive tree should be as common here as it is in the old world, especially as it is the emblem of peace. My old friend, Dominick Lynch, sir, the wine-merchant, the only *great* wine-merchant we ever had, sir, imported the finest oil, sir, from Lucca, known even to this day as 'Lynch's Oil.' He it was who made Château Margaux and the Italian opera, popular, sir, in this great metropolis. Poor Dom! Well, sir, I suppose you know all about the olive tree?"

"On the contrary, very little."

2

"Well, the olive is as easily propagated as the willow. You must go boldly to work, however, and cut off a limb of the tree, as big as my arm, and plant that. No twig, sir. In three years it will bear; in five years it will have a full crop; in ten years it will be in perfection. If you plant a slip, it will take twenty years or more to mature. Its mode of bearing is biennial, and you can prune it every other year, and plant the cuttings. Longworth ought to take up the olive, sir; and he might have a wreath to put around his head, as he deserves. Well, my learned friend, when the olive is ripe—the fruit I mean—it is of a deep violet color. Those we get in bottles are plucked while they are green. The plums are put between two circular mill-stones—the upper one convex, the lower one concave; the fruit is thus crushed, and afterward put into a press, and the oil is extracted by means of a powerful lever. That is all, sir; an oil-press is not a very handsome article to look at; but in the South, I think it would be serviceable at least; butter there is not always of the best quality in summer; and olive oil would be a delightful substitute."

"What of French and Spanish oil, Doctor?"

"Spanish oil is very good, sir. So is French; we get little of the Italian oil now. The oil of Aix, near Marseilles, is of superior quality; but that does not come to our market. Lately I have used the oil of Bordeaux in place of the Italian; it is very fine. But speaking of olive oil, let me tell you an anecdote of my friend Godey,

of Philadelphia, of the *Ladies' Book*, sir, the best hearted man of that name in the world. Well, sir, Godey had
a new servant-girl; I never knew any body that didn't
have a *new* servant-girl! Well, sir, Godey had a dinner-
party in early spring, when lettuce is a rarity, and of
course he had lettuce. He is a capital hand at a salad,
and so he dressed it. The guests ate it; and—sir—well,
sir, I must hasten to the end of the story. Said Godey
to the new girl next morning: 'What has become of that
bottle of castor-oil I gave you to put away yesterday
morning?' 'Sure,' said she, '*you said it was castor-oil,
and I put it in the castor.*' 'Well,' said Godey, 'I
thought so.'"

IV.

Chocolate and Cocoa.

"How is it, Doctor," said we over our matutinal, but unusual cup of chocolate, "how is it that drinking chocolate produces a headache with many persons who can eat chocolate bon-bons by the quantity with impunity!" "My learned friend," said Dr. Bushwhacker, rousing up and shaking his mane, "I will tell you all about it. Chocolate, or as the great Linnæus used to call it, '*Theo broma*'—food for the gods—is a most peculiar preparation. It is made of the berries of the cacao, sir, a small tree indigenous to South America. We misname the berries cocoa, because the *jicaras*, or native cups in which the cocoa was drunk by the Mexicans, were made of the small end of the cocoa-nut. The tree, sir, bears a beautiful rose-colored blossom, and that produces a long pod, resembling our cucumber; in that pod we find the cacao imbedded—a multitude of oval pits, about the size of shelled almonds, and surrounded with a white acid pulp. Now, sir, this pulp produces a very refreshing drink in the tropics, called *vino cacao*, or cacao-wine, which is more esteemed there than the beverage we make from the berries."

"But, Doctor, how about the headache?"

20

"Sir," said the Doctor, "I am getting to that. If you take a pair of compasses, and put the right leg in the middle of the Madeira River, one of the tributaries of the majestic Amazon, and extend the other to Caracas, then sweep it round in a circle, you will embrace within that the native land of the cacao. It grows, sir, from Venezuela to the Pampas of Buenos Ayres, an extent of country more beautiful, vaster, and of less importance than any other territory on the habitable globe. Well, sir, this plant, which, from its oleaginous properties, seems suitable to supply the want of animal food, is expressly adapted for that country. 'He who has drank one cup,' says Fernando Cortez, 'can travel a whole day without any other food.' Now, sir, we must not believe this altogether; but the value of this liquid nutriment for those who have to cross the Llanos of the north, or the Pampas of the south, is not to be lightly estimated."

"But the headache, Doctor?"

"Chocolate," continued Dr. Bushwhacker, "is made of the cacao berries, slightly roasted and triturated in water; a certain degree of heat is necessary in its preparation. The best we have comes from Caracas, it is of a light brown color, and quite expensive, sometimes two or three dollars a pound. The ordinary chocolate we import from France, Spain, Germany, and the West Indies, is a mixture of cacao with sago, rice, sugar, and other articles, flavored with cinnamon or vanilla, the latter being deleterious on account of its effects upon the nervous sys-

tem. How much Caracas cacao is used here I do not
know, but I presume Pará furnishes our manufacturers
with their principal supplies. The quantity of cacao that
comes here in its native state is very great, compared
with the manufactured article, the chocolate ; we import
one hundred and seventy thousand dollars' worth of the
one, against a little over two thousand dollars' worth of
the other."

"But the headache, Doctor ? What is the reason that
liquid choco——"

"Sir," replied Dr. Bushwhacker, drawing himself up
with cast-iron dignity, "if I interrupted you as often as
you interrupt me, that question would be answered some
time after the allies take Sebastopol. Chocolate was
introduced into Spain by Fernando Cortez ; to this day
it is in Spain what coffee is to France, or tea to England,
the pet beverage of all classes of people who can afford
it. It was introduced into England simultaneously with
coffee, just before the restoration of King Charles the
Second. Then it was prepared for the table by merely
mixing it with hot water, no milk, sir. Pope alludes to
it in the Rape of the Lock. 'Whatever spirit, careless
of his charge, his post neglects,'

> 'In fumes of burning chocolate shall glow,
> And tremble at the sea that froths below.'

The Spaniards, sir, do not use milk in preparing it, nor
do the **South Americans**. By the way, thirty years ago,

my friend, Col. Duane, of Philadelphia, published a book
on Colombia, which is highly interesting; so, too, you will
find Zea's Colombia of the same period; Pazo's Letters
to Henry Clay, written in 1819; Depon's Voyages in the
early part of this century; and the still more interesting
voyages of Don George Juan, and Don Antonio de Ulloa,
in 1735. Then there is Hippisly's Narrative, Brown's
Itinerary, and many other books, my learned friend, that
will tell you about the cacao. In that country, where
meat is not abundant, a cup of chocolate supplies the
necessary nutriment, and a breakfast of cacao and fruit,
sir, is satisfying and delicious. Arbuthnot says it is rich,
alimentary, and anodyne."

"But the headache, Doctor?"

"In Spain," continued the Doctor, it is served up in
beautiful cups of fillagree work, made in the shape of
tulips or lilies, with leaves that fold over the top by
touching a spring. These leaves are to protect it from
the flies. The ladies are so fond of it that they have it
sent after them to church; this the bishops interdicted
for a while, but that only made it more desirable."

"But what are its peculiar properties, Doctor?"

"Tea, my learned friend," replied the Doctor, curtly,
"inspires scandal and sentiment; coffee excites the imagination; but chocolate, sir, is aphrodisiac!"

V

Notables and Potables.

"My dear learned friend," said Dr. Bush-whacker, putting down his half-empty goblet of claret, "that is the finest wine I ever tasted. A man, sir, should go down on his knees when he drinks such wine ; it inspires me, sir, with humility and devotion. Six months' retirement and study, with a liberal allowance of claret like that would induce an epic poem, sir !"

"Retirement and study would do much, Doctor ; but as for the claret I have my doubts. France, with all her clarets, has no great poet."

"Sir," replied Doctor Bushwhacker, "France has Corneille, Racine, Molière !"

"True."

"La Fontaine, Voltaire, and Boileau."

"True."

"Jongleurs, Troubadours, Trouveres, without number, sir !"

"I know it."

"Béranger, Lamartine, Victor Hugo, and—what is the name of that barber-poet ?—ah ! Jasmin."

" Yes, Jasmin."

" And," continued the Doctor, " there was Du Bartas, sir, who wrote the ' Divine Week' and the ' Battle of Ivry,' sir !"

" Yes, sir."

" Claret," said Dr. Bushwhacker significantly.

" Great thing for wit, Doctor !"

" My dear learned friend, it is," replied the Doctor, emptying his goblet, and giving a triumphant snort, "and for poetry, too."

" How is it, then, that with all her great poets, France has not produced a great poem ?"

" Sir," asked Dr. Bushwhacker, " did you ever read the Œdipe of Corneille ?"

" No, sir."

" Then I would advise you to read it, sir."

" My learned friend," continued Dr. Bushwhacker, after an impressive pause, " I have a theory that certain wines produce certain effects upon the mind. I believe, sir, that if I were to come in upon a dinner-party about the time when conversation had become luminous and choral, I could easily tell whether Claret, Champagne, Sherry, Madeira, Burgundy, Port, or Punch, had been the prevailing potable. Yes, sir, and no doubt a skillful critic could determine, after a careful analysis of the subject, upon what drink, sir, a poem was written. Yes, sir, or tell a claret couplet from a sherry couplet, sir, or distinguish the flavor of Port in one stanza, and Madeira in another, from internal evidence, sir."

" Suppose, Doctor, the poet were a water-drinker ?"

"My dear learned friend," replied the Doctor vehemently, " if you can find in the whole range of literature —and I will go farther than that—if you can find in the whole range of intelligence, either poet, statesman, orator, artist, hero, or divine, who was a water-drinker, and worth one (excuse me) curse! then, sir, I will renounce the practice of my profession, and occupy my time in a water-cure establishment. On the contrary, look at the *illustrious writers* of all ages and nations, sir; look at Homer. There is no end to the juncketings in the Iliad, sir ; and the Greek heaven, sir, is pretty well supplied with every thing else but water, I believe.

> ——' This did to laughter cheer
> White-wristed Juno, who now took a cup of him, and smiled,
> The sweet peace-making draught went round, and lame Ephaistus
> Nectar to all the other gods. A laughter never left,   [filled
> Shook all the blessed deities, to see the lame so deft
> At the cup service. All that day, even till the sun went down,
> They banqueted; and had such cheer as did their wishes crown.' "

" What was Homer's peculiar tipple, Doctor ?"

" The wine of Chios, sir, undoubtedly. In this island, it is said, the first wines were made by Œnopion, son of Bacchus ; and here, too, it is said Homer was born. I believe both, sir. From the island of Chios came the first wine and the first epic, sir ; hand in hand they came into the world, and hand in hand they will go out of it. sir !"

"The Romans, Doctor, were great wine-drinkers."

"Yes, my learned friend. Falernian and Massic, sir, inspired Virgil and Horace, and the poets have made the wines immortal. Martial praises his native wine of Tarragonia, sir ; he was an old sherry drinker. And had the Italian vine, sir, perished with the Roman Empire, I have my doubts whether Dante, Pulci, Tasso, Petrarch, Boïardo, and Ariosto would have been what they now are in the eyes of an admiring posterity. Yes, sir, and there is Redi, too ! Why, the whole of Italy is in his '*Bacco in Toscana.*' "

"What wine do you suppose Shakspeare preferred, Doctor ?"

"Sack ! my learned friend—dry Sherry or Canary, sir. All the poets of the Elizabethan age, sir, were sack-drinkers—Ben Johnson, Beaumont, Fletcher, Marlowe, Raleigh, Chapman, Spencer, Sydney—so, too, was Herrick, as he says :

> ' Thy Iles shall lack
> Grapes, before Herrick leave Canarie Sack.'

and the other writers of his time, sir—Carew, Wither, Cowley, Waller, Crashaw, Broome—

> ' All worldly care is Madness ;
> But Sack and good Chear
> Will, in spite of our fear,
> Inspire our Souls with Gladness.'

That was the burthen of a song in the time of the Rump, sir! It was a 'Rump and dozen' in those days, my learned friend."

"One writer of that period was an exception, Doctor."

"What writer, sir?"

"Milton."

"Died of the gout, sir—died of the gout, sir. Milton, my dear friend, died of the gout."

"Cervantes was a Sherry-drinker, Doctor?"

"Of course, my learned friend. And, no doubt, the 'Val de Peñas' of La Mancha was a favorite beverage with him. But, sir," continued Dr. Bushwhacker suddenly, sitting upright and holding his head like a poised avalanche, "by speaking of Cervantes, sir, you have put a keystone into the arch of my theory, sir. The Elizabethan era should be called the age of Sack, sir. Look at those two great writers, Shakspeare and Cervantes, each a transcendant genius, sir; both living at the same time, sir; both dying on the same day, sir—on the 23d of April, 1616."

"Well, Doctor?"

"And both drinking Sack, sir, or Sherry, constantly. 'If I had a thousand sons, the first human principle I would teach them should be, to forswear thin potations, and to addict themselves to Sack.' Shakspeare, sir! King Henry Fourth, part second, act fourth, scene third, sir!"

"How long did this golden age of Sack continue, Doctor?"

"Until Charles the Second returned from France, and brought Claret into fashion. You can see the light, delicate, fanciful potable, sir, in the literature of this period as plain as sunlight. Next came the age of Port, sir, in Queen Anne's reign."

"Ah! I remember, the Methuen treaty."

"Yes, sir, the treaty of 1703. Port was encouraged by low duties, and lighter and better wines of other countries interdicted by enormous imposts, and in consequence we have a new school of literature, sir. The imaginative, the nervous, the pathetic, the humorous, and the sublime departed with the age of Sack; the gay, the witty, the amorous, and the fanciful, with the age of Claret; and the artificial, the critical, the satirical, and the common-place arose, sir, with the age of Port! But bless my heart," said Doctor Bushwhacker, rising and looking at his watch, "I must look after my patients. The next time we meet we will have a talk over modern wines and authors, and that will be more interesting, I dare say."

Notables and Potables=Continued.

"The last discourse we had, my learned friend," said Dr. Bushwhacker, "was about wine and wisdom. What shall be the next?"

"Pardon me, Doctor, we are not yet through with

that. We reached Port and Queen Anne; what followed after the age of Pope and Addison?"

"The prohibition of wine, sir," replied the Doctor, solemnly, "led to the substitution of spirits. You see how Hogarth, in his immortal pictures, shows its progress in Gin Lane. Well, sir, if you wish to see how intimate are the relations between drinking and thinking, mark the host of clever literary vagabonds of this period. Genius in rags, sir; genius with immortal thoughts in his brain and no crown to his hat; Pegassus, with every thing but his wings, in the pawnbroker's shop. The long exhausting toil of literary occupation, which needs a *natural* stimulant, such as wine, (for men of sedentary habits must have it, sir,) was relieved by stronger stimulants, because they were cheaper. And now, sir, mark the two great geniuses of the middle of the last century, Fielding and Smollett; see the wonderful power of those writers, and observe the characteristic coarseness of their works, and what else is there to say ' to point a moral,' farther, than that Smollett, with a shattered constitution, went to Leghorn, to die there; and Fielding, with a shattered constitution, went to Lisbon, to die there. Fielding, at the age of 47, and Smollett at the age of 50, sir."

"What would you infer from that, Doctor?"

"Sir," replied the Doctor, "I leave you to draw the inference. Now, sir, we come to another epoch. A period, sir, of great mental brilliancy, and I wish you to observe that fine wine drinking had again become fashionable. Claret was monstrously expensive, but claret was the mode. Now, sir, we have Fox, and Pitt, and Sheridan, and Burke, and Chesterfield, and Garrick, and Sir Joshua Reynolds, and Goldsmith. And among this brilliant cluster there stands out conspicuous a remarkable figure. Not that he was greater than these, not that his genius was superior, nor his wisdom more profound, yet still the most conspicuous figure in the group was ——"

"Dr. Samuel Johnson."

"Dr. Jamuel Johnson," echoed Dr. Bushwhacker. "Did you ever know, sir, leaving out a few of our prominent hydrophobists, a man so eminent for invective, asperity, bitterness, insolence, dogmatic assumption, and gluttony, as the Ursa Major of English literature? And, sir, he was a total abstinent. To use his own words: 'I now no more think of drinking wine than a horse does. The wine upon the table is no more for me than for the dog who is under the table.' But he could drink, sir, twenty-three cups of tea at poor Mrs. Thrale's table at a sitting, until four o'clock in the morning, sir, which may be set down as a fair sample of teetotal debauchery, my learned friend."

"Dr. Johnson was a very good hearted man, I believe."

"A good man, sir, a good man, sir. His charity, his candor, his tenderness, his attachment to his friends, his love of the poor, his rigid honesty, his piety, and his filial affection, were wonderful, sir, We all love *this* Samuel

Johnson. But, sir, there was also another character; an irritable, uncouth, imperious, ill-tempered, gluttonous, rude, prejudiced, intolerant, violent, unsparing old cynic; and *this* Samuel Johnson we do not love. Sir, human nature has scarcely formed a character so disproportionate. He was a great man, sir, and a great bear, sir."

"I thought you said no *water* drinker ever was a great man, Doctor?"

"My learned friend," replied the Doctor, growing slightly purple, "Dr. Samuel Johnson was a *tea drinker*, and used to be a wine drinker! But hand me the Maderia, if you please, and a handful of filberts. At the next dinner we will talk of the writers of this century. What is this wine?"

"Virginia Reserve, Doctor."

"Then we will drink it, sir; Virginia is a noble State, and it is full of noble men—"

"And women, Doctor."

"God bless you, my dear friend—and women!"

Notables and Potables=Continued.

"What do you think of whiskey-punch, Doctor, as a potable?"

"Bless my heart!" said the Doctor, shaking his bushy mane, "by all means; I never refuse it."

(*Enter a tray, two lemons, hot water, a silver sugar bowl, and the Islay.*)

"Punch," said Doctor Bushwhacker, "was the chief inspirer of the hearty, homely, natural, vigorous writers of this century. You see how the great Sir Walter used it, sir; there is a touch of 'mountain dew' in his tenderest productions, sir; the Heart of Mid-Lothian could never have been written by a cold-water drinker—no, sir; nor was it. I may even go a little farther back, to a more unfortunate child of genius—Burns, sir! Robert of Ayrshire loved the *barley broo*—'not wisely, but too well'—for himself; he was improvident; but then he made posterity rich. (A little more of the Islay; thank you.")

"Byron, Doctor?"

"Drank gin; that we know pretty well, I believe, my learned friend. There is a touch of juniper in all Bryon—a mixture of the bitter and the aromatic."

"And Coleridge?"

"Coleridge," said the Doctor, gravely, with a sort of emphatic spill of the hot fluid, "illustrates my theory in a remarkable manner, sir—Coleridge and De Quincey, both. What idea do you have of the Vision of Kubla Khan, and the Suspiria de Profundis, taken together? My learned friend, he begins to dream who is absorbed in the pages of either: the world, yea, the great globe itself, becomes intangible; he is floating away, on a sea of ether, in space more illimitable than human thought could scan before; his vision is dilated, yet undefined; the procession of time sweeps on, measured by centuries;

events accumulate with supernatural aggregation; the
scenery by which he is surrounded has surpassed sublimi-
ty itself, and he listens to the river that runs

'——through caverns, *measureless to man*,
Down to a SUNLESS sea.'

"Well, Doctor?"

"OPIUM, sir!" replied the Doctor, with awful solem-
nity.

"What of Charles Lamb, Doctor?"

"Lamb? Dear Charles, has certainly lisped of hot gin
and water in his inimitable letters," replied the Doctor,
"or, as he would say, '*hot water*, with a s-s-s-entiment
of gin.'"

"That sounds Lambish, Doctor."

"My learned friend," replied Dr. Bushwhacker, "I
know it; I have got Charles Lamb by heart, sir. By the
way, a new anecdote of Elia: he had a friend one night
at No. 4 Inner Temple Lane; negus was the potable of
the evening, from tenderness to Mary's feelings, who
sometimes shook her sisterly head at the 's-s-s-entiment.'
It seems a poor cur dog had attracted the attention of the
gentle-hearted Charles that day, and he had invited him
in, fed him, and tied him up slightly in the little yard
back of the house. Charles was talking in his phosphro-
resent way over the negus, when Mary interrupted him:
Charles, that dog yelps so.' Elia flashed on. 'Charles,
that dog—' 'What i-i-is it, Mary? Oh! the dog?

He-he-he-he's enjoying him-s-s-self.' 'Enjoying himself,
Charles?' 'Ye-ye-yes—as well as he can with 'whine and
water.'"

"Capital story, Doctor. What of the Laureate?"

"In reading Southey," replied Doctor Bushwhacker,
"you feel the want of the rare old vinous smack peculiar to the writings of authors of eminence, sir. I may
say the same, too, of Wordsworth. Both were tolerably
abstinent; but Southey had his wine-cellar at Greta Hall,
and Wordsworth, in celebrating his first visit to the
rooms once occupied by Milton at Christ College, was a
little overcome, sir, by—a—*his visit, sir.* Southey, in his
personal character, manners, and habits, must have re-
sembled our dear Henry Inman, sir."

"And Hazlitt?"

"Misanthropic, cynical, Hazlitt, sir, used to drink
black tea, sir, of the intensest strength. He is another
illustration of my theory, sir."

"And Keats?"

"Read Keats over, my learned friend; and if you can
unlatch the tendrils of the vine from any of 'his super-
exquisite poems, great or small, then sir, I will bury my
lancet. What a delicate taste for wine he must have had!"

"And Shelley, Doctor?"

"My dear friend," said the Doctor, rising, and upset-
ting his tumbler, "Shelley never understood the human
aspect of existence. I fear me he was not a wine-drinker.
Suppose we say, or admit he was a solitary exception?"

"Do you know," said Dr. Bushwhacker, as he stretched out his full glass to be touched, "how this custom originated? — this ringing of wine-bells or kissing of beakers, sir?"

We replied in the negative.

"Then, sir, I will tell you," replied the Doctor. "It was the invention of a learned French philosopher, to illustrate the five senses. The beautiful color of wine delights the eye—*seeing*, the delicate boquet gratifies the nose—*smelling*, the cool glass suggests a pleasure to the fingers—*feeling*, and, sir, by drinking it we gratify exquisitely—the *taste*. Now, sir, touch glasses for the finest chime in the world, that rings out good fellowship, sir, and we have the fifth sense—*hearing*."

"Quite a little poem, Doctor, in five lines."

"Put it in verse, sir, put it in verse—I give you the idea."

"*Appropos*, Doctor, I have a German song here, translated by a friend: Let me read it to you." (*Editor reads.*)

"LOVE, SONG, AND WINE.

DEAR FREDERICUS: A. Walther writ this in 'quaint old sounding German.' It is done into English by your friend,   HUGH PYNNSAURRT.

Through the gloom of this sad life of ours,
    Three glorious planets still shine,
Serene from the azure of heaven,
    And men call them Love, Song, and Wine.

In the dear voice of love all the passion
    Of a trusting and earnest heart lies;
And pleasure by love grows immortal,
    While sorrow faints, withers, and dies.

Then wine gives a courage to passion,
    Inspires the melodious art,
And reddens the gold of the sunlight
    That streams o'er the May of the heart,

But song is most noble of all these;
    To mortals it adds the divine;
It thrills through our hearts like a passion,
    And glows through our senses like wine.

Then quench all the rest of the planets,
    Bid the golden-rayed stars cease to shine;
We'll not miss them so long as God leaves us
    Those heart-stars of Love, Song, and Wine."

"Excellent!" said the Doctor, shaking his bushy head. "By the way, what grand old songs those Rhine songs are! And the vineyards of the Rhine are reflected in the songs as they are in the river. 'O! the pride of the German heart is this noble River! and right it is; for of the rivers of this beautiful earth, there is none so beautiful as this. There is hardly a league of its whole course, from its cradle in the snowy Alps to its grave in the sands of Holland, which boasts not its peculiar charms. By heavens! if I were a German, I would be proud of it, too; and of the clustering grapes that hang about its temples, as it reels onwards through vineyards in a triumphal march, like Bacchus, crowned and drunken.' There, sir, what do you think of that?"

"Grand, Doctor, like the triumphant chanting of an organ. Who wrote it?"

"Henry Wadsworth Longfellow, sir !Hyperion, sir, Read it over, and get it by heart."

"The German writers all use the wines of Fatherland, Doctor."

"Nearly all, from Martin Luther down. I say nearly all—Goethe was an exception. The courtly Goethe used to drink the fine Burgundies and Bordeaux of France. But Schiller, sir, was a Rhine-wine drinker. In fact his writing-table was always supplied with the golden potable of the Rhine. Now, sir, we see between these two men of eminent genius, two separate and distinguishing characteristics. Goethe was different from all other German poets—but Schiller was above all other German poets, including Goethe himself."

VI.

A Peep into a Salad-Bowl.

"My dear, learned friend," said the Doctor, "a Bowl of Lettuce is the Venus of the dinner table! It rises upon the sight cool, moist and beautiful, like that very imprudent lady coming out of the sea, sir! And to complete the image, sir, neither should be dressed too much!"

When Dr. Bushwhacker had issued this observation, he drew himself up in a very portly manner, as if he felt called upon to defend himself as well as his image. Then, after a short pause, he broke—silence.

"*Lactuca*, or lettuce, is one of the most common vegetables in the world; it has been known, sir, from time immemorial; it was as common, sir, on the tables of the ancients as it is now, and was eaten in the same way, sir, dressed with oil and vinegar. We get, sir, from Athenæus some idea of the condiments used: not all of these contributed to make a salad, but it shows they had the materials:

'Dried grapes, and salt, and eke new wine
Newly boiled down, and asafœtida, (pah!)
And cheese, and thyme, and sesame, (open sesame,)
And nitre too, and cummin-seed,
And sumach, honey, and majorum,

And herbs, and vinegar, and oil,
And sauce of onions, mustard and capers mixed,
And parsley, capers too, and eggs,
And lime, and cardimums, and th' acid juice
Which comes from the green fig-tree ; besides lard,
And eggs and honey, and flour wrapped in fig-leaves,
And all compounded in one savory force-meat.'

They had pepper too.   Ophelian says:

' Pepper from Lybya take, and frankincense.'

So, sir, if you had dined with Alcibiades, no doubt he would have dressed a salad for you with Samian oil, and Sphettian vinegar, sir, pepper from Lybia, and salt from —ah—hm—"

" Attica, doctor."

"Attica, my learned friend; thank you.   Now, sir, there was one thing the ancients did with lettuce which we do not do.   They boiled it, sir, and served it up like asparagus; so, too, did they with cucumbers—a couple of indigestible dishes they were, no doubt.   Lettuce, my dear friend, should have a quick growth, in the first place, to be good; it should have a rich mould, sir, that it may spring up quickly, so as to be tender and crisp.   Then, sir, it should be *new-plucked*, carried from the garden a few minutes before it is placed upon the table.   I would suggest a parasol, sir, to keep the leaves cool until it reaches the shadow of within-doors.   Then, sir, it must be washed—mind you—ice-water!   Then place it upon the table—what Corinthian ornament more perfect and symmetrical.   Now, sir, comes the important part, the DRESSING.   'To dress a salad,' says the learned Petrus

Petronius, 'you must have a prodigal to furnish the oil, a counselor to dispense the salt, a miser to dole out the vinegar, and a madman to stir it.' Commit that to memory, my learned friend."

"It is down, Doctor." (*Tablets.*)

"Let me show you," continued Dr. Bushwhacker, "how to dress a salad. Take a small spoonful of salt, thus: twice the quantity of mustard—'Durham'—thus: incorporate: pour a slender stream of oil from the cruet, so: gently mix and increase the action by degrees," (head of hair in commotion, and face brilliant in color;) "dear me! it is very warm—now, sir, oil in abundance, so; a dash of vinegar, very light, like the last touches of the artist; and, sir, we have the dressing. Now, take up the lettuce by the stalk! Break off the leaves—leaf by leaf—shake off the water, replace it in the salad-bowl, pepper it slightly, pour on the dressing, and there you have it, sir."

"Doctor, is that orthodox?"

"Sir," replied Dr. Bushwhacker, holding the boxwood spoon in one hand and the box-wood fork in the other; "the eyes of thirty centuries are looking down upon me. I know that Frenchmen will sprinkle the lettuce with oil until it is thorougly saturated; then, sir, a little pepper; then, sir, salt or not, as it happens; then, sir, *vinaigre* by the drop—all very well. Our people, sir, in the State of New Jersey, will dress it with salt, vinegar, and pepper—perfectly barbarous, my learned friend; then comes

the elaborate Englishman ; and our Pennsylvania friend,
the Rev. Sidney Smith, sir, gives us a recipe in verse,
that shows how they do it there, and at the same time,
exhibits the deplorable ignorance of that very peculiar
people.   I quote from memory, sir:

> Two large potatoes, passed through kitchen sieve
> Smoothness and softness to the salad give ;
> Of mordant mustard add a single spoon,
> Distrust the condiment that bites too soon,
> But deem it not, Lady of herbs, a fault
> To add a double quantity of salt.
> Four times the spoon with oil of Lucca crown,
> And twice with vinegar procured from town ;
> True flavor needs it, and your poet begs
> The pounded yellow of two well-boiled eggs.
> Let onion atoms lurk within the bowl,
> And, scarce suspected, animate the whole.
> Then lastly in the flavored compound toss
> One magic spoonful of anchovy sauce.
> O great and glorious! O herbaceous treat!
> 'T would tempt the dying anchorite to eat ;
> Back to the world he'd turn his weary soul,
> And plunge his fingers in the Salad Bowl !'

Now, sir, I have *tried* that, and a compound more execra-
ble is not to be thought of. No, sir!   Take some of my
salad, and see if you do not dream afterwards of the
Greek mythology."

VII.

Madame Follet.

"My dear friend," said the Doctor, holding his cup in the left hand thumb and forefinger, with the other three fingers stretched out over the rest of the table, "I never inhale the fragrance of coffee without thinking of the old fashioned coffee pot, or 'Madame Follet,' as dear Miss Bremer used to call it. Do you know, sir—and I suppose you know every thing—do you know, sir, there are a great many old fashioned people in the world?"

We replied, the fact was not to be disputed.

"Old fashioned people, sir; old fashioned in dress, in speech, in politeness, in ideas, in every thing. And, sir, not long since, I had occasion to visit two old ladies, sir; I went down stairs to the basement dining room, sir, without ceremony, sir, and there I found the antiquated virgins over their coffee, sir; and in the middle of the table there was the old fashioned tin coffee pot, sir, scoured as bright as sand could make it, with a great big superannuated spout, and a great broad backed handle, sir, and a great big, broad bottom, sir, as broad, sir, as

the top of the great bell crowned hat I used to wear
when I went to visit them as a spruce young buck, in the
year eighteen hundred and twenty, sir." Here the Doctor's spectacles fairly glistened again.

" Well, Doctor ?"

" Sir," replied Dr. Bushwhacker, " there was plenty
of silver in the cupboard, plenty ; great pots, and coffee
urns of solid metal, sir, with massive handles to match ;
but they were so old fashioned as to prefer the old,
scoured, broad bottomed tin pot, sir, and with reason,
too, sir."

" Give us the reason, thereof, Doctor, if you please."

" Well, sir, one of the sisters apologized for the coffee
pot in a still, small sort of a voice, a little cracked and
chipped by constant use, and said, the reason why they
drank their coffee out of that pot was *because it never
seemed to taste so well out of any thing else.*"

" Why not, Doctor ?"

" Why not ? Easily enough explained, sir ; we never
make coffee in a silver urn, and when we pour it from the
vessel in which it is made into another, we lose half the
aroma, sir. Coffee is of most delicate and choice flavor,
sir ; very few know how to make it or to use it. The
proper way to make good coffee, sir, is to roast it carefully in a cylinder over a charcoal fire, until it is of a light
brown color ; then the cylinder should be taken off the
fire and turned gently until the berries are thoroughly
cooled. The best part of the aroma is dissipated, sir, by

the abominable practice of turning out the coffee in an open dish so soon as it is roasted. Why, sir, any body can see that the finest part of it escapes; you can smell it, sir, in every crack and corner of the house. When cooled, it should be put into a mortar and beat to powder. A coffee mill only cracks the grains, but a mortar pounds out the essential oil. Then, sir, put it into an old fashioned tin coffee pot, pour on the hot water, stand it over a fire, not too hot; let it simmer *gently*. If your fire is too hot, it will burn the coffee and spoil it. Then, sir, take Madam Follett fresh from the fire, stand her on the table, and if you want an appreciative friend, send for me!"

"What kind of coffee is the best, Doctor?"

"Mocha, sir, from Arabia Felix. The first Mocha coffee that ever reached the Land of the Free and the Home of the Brave direct, sir, came in a ship belonging to Captain Derby, of Salem, in the year 1801."

"When was coffee first used in Europe, Doctor?"

"That, my learned friend, is one of 'the two or three things to suggest conversation at the tea table,' as our friend Willis has it. It is a matter of dispute, my learned friend, and it will probably be settled after the commentators have agreed upon the proper way of spelling the name of Shakspeare, Shaksper, Shagsper, or whatever you call him."

"How early was coffee in use in the world?"

"Sherbaddin, an Arab author, asserts that the first man who drank coffee was a certain Mufti, of Aden, who

lived in the ninth century of the Hegira, about the year
1500, my learned friend. So says Dr. Doran. The popular tradition is, that the superior of a Dervish community, observing the effects of coffee berries, when eaten
by some goats, rendering them more lively and skittish
than before, prescribed it for the brotherhood, in order
to cure them of drowsiness and indolence. Dickens, in
Household Words, gives a capital account of the old coffee houses of London. By the way, there is an account,
also, in *Table Traits*. Here is the book.

'Lend me thine ears.'—*Shagsper.*

'The coffee houses of England take precedence of
those of France, though the latter have more enduringly
flourished. In 1652, a Greek, in the service of an English Turkey merchant, opened a house in London. ' I
have discovered his hand bill,' says Mr. Disraeli, 'in
which he sets forth the virtue of the coffee drink, first
publiquely made and sold in England, by Pasqua Rosee,
of St. Michael's Alley, Cornhill, at the sign of his own
head.' Mr. Peter Cunningham cites a MS. of Oldys' in
his possession, in which some fuller details of much interest are given. Oldys says: ' The first use of coffee in
England was known in 1657, when Mr. Daniel Edwards,
a Turkey merchant, brought from Smyrna to London one
Pasqua Rosee, a Ragusan youth, who prepared this drink
for him every morning. But the novelty thereof drawing
too much company to him, he allowed his said servant,
with another of his son-in-law's, to sell it publicly; and
they set up the first coffee house in London, in St. Michael's Alley, Cornhill. But they separating, Pasqua
kept in the house; and he who had been his partner ob-
tained leave to pitch a tent, and sell the liquor, in St.

Michael's church yard.' Aubrey, in his *Anecdotes*, states that the first vender of coffee in London was one Bowman, coachman to a Turkey merchant, named Hodges, who was the father-in-law of Edwards, and the partner of Pasqua, who got into difficulties, partly by his not being a freeman, and who left the country. Bowman was not only patronized, but a magnificent contribution of one thousand sixpences was presented to him, wherewith he made great improvements in his coffee house. Bowman took an apprentice, (Paynter,) who soon learnt the mystery, and in four years set up for himself. The coffee houses soon became numerous; the principal were Farres', the Rainbow, at the Inner Temple Gate, and John's, in Fuller's Rents.'

"There, sir; and now, my learned friend, I must pay a visit to that charming lady, Mrs. Potiphar, who is suffering severely with a neuralgia."

VIII.

Old Phrases.

"For my part," said the Doctor, "I do not see how we could get along without them. The old phrases, the idioms, the apothegms of a people are the gold and silver coins of their language, bearing a proportionate value, as many hundred times, to the common stock of words, as these do to the copper currency. Sir, if you will get the 'Lessons on Proverbs,' by Richard Chenevix Trench, you will find you have a sub-treasury of wisdom, my learned friend."

"Do you not think, Doctor, there is a coarseness in familiar proverbs that diminishes their value in polite society?"

"No, sir, I do not think so," replied the Doctor vehemently. "To be sure, there may be, here and there one in which an allusion might offend a sensitive mind; but, generally speaking, they are rather robust, instead of coarse, strong without being indelicate. Cervantes felicitously calls them '*Sentencias brevas sacadas de la luenga y discreta experiencia*'—short sentences drawn from long and wise experience. Common enough are they among

uneducated people, but not the less valuable for that reason, sir; proverbs may be called the *literature of the
illiterate*—another mouthful of the Mumm, sir—thank
you."

"How do you like that wine, Doctor?"

"Grand, sir; glorious, sir; 'Mumm's the word,' sir.
If Shakspeare were living, sir, he would forswear sack,
and say '*Mumm*'—'a jewel of a wine, sir—Jewel
Mumm."

"The phrase you have just used, Doctor, is a common
one."

"'Mumm's the word?' True, my learned friend. Dr.
Johnson, that stupendous lexicographer, remarks of the
word mumm, it may be observed that when it is pronounced it leaves the lips closed, thus," (lips in sculptured
silence.)

"How did the phrase originate, Doctor?"

"That, sir, is a question I can not answer. There are
phrases, sir, beyond the scope of records, written or
printed, so old, sir, that, to use the words of our friend
Blackstone, ' the memory of man runneth not to the contrary'—they were *always* in use. Others we can trace at
once to their originals; such as, 'How we apples swim,'
to a fable in Æsop; or, 'To see ourselves as others see
us,' to a poem of Burns; there are legions of phrases
from the Bible, not one of which inculcates a sentiment
not divine in its humanity; there are scores from Shakspeare, scores from Pope, scores from Young, some from

3

Byron, from Milton, Cowper, Thomson, Campbell, Gold-
smith, Spenser, Addison, Congreve, Prior, Sir Philip
Sidney, Gray, Collins, Cowley, our own poets, sir—and
Daniel Webster, sir, Halleck and Irving."

"There is no fear of a language, Doctor, in which such
coin is current."

"No, sir; nor of a people! But there are other
phrases which, to the undisciplined ear, seem coarse and
vulgar, yet involving a story clever enough in itself to be
preserved."

"For instance?"

"For instance, 'The gray mare is the better horse.'
We know very well the line is in Prior's Epilogue to
Lucius; but the story from which the phrase is derived
is something like this: A gentleman, who had seen the
world, one day gave his eldest son a span of horses, a
chariot, and a basket of eggs. 'Do you,' said he to the
boy, 'travel upon the high road until you come to the
first house in which there is a married couple. If you
find the husband is the master there, give him one of the
horses. If, on the contrary, the wife is the ruler, give
her an egg. Return at once if you part with a horse,
but do not come back so long as you keep both horses,
and there is an egg remaining.' Away went the boy full
of his mission, and just beyond the borders of his father's
estate lo! a modest cottage. He alighted from the chariot and knocked at the door. The good wife opened it
for him and curtesied. 'Is your husband at home?'

'No ;' but she would call him from the hay field. In he came, wiping his brows. The young man told them his errand. 'Why,' said the wife, bridling and rolling the corner of her apron, 'I always do as John wants me to do; he is my master—an't you, John?' To which John replied, 'Yes.' 'Then,' said the boy, 'I am to give you a horse; which will you take?' 'I think,' said John, 'as how that bay gelding seems to be the one as would suit me the best.' 'If we have a *choice*, husband,' said the wife, '*I* think the gray mare will suit us better.' 'No,' replied John, 'the bay for me; he is more square in front, and his legs are better.' 'Now,' said the wife, 'I don't think so; the gray mare is the better horse; and I shall never be contented unless I get that one.' 'Well,' said John, 'if your mind is sot on it, I'll give up; we'll take the gray mare.' 'Thank you,' said the boy; 'allow me to give you an egg from this basket; it is a nice fresh one, and you can boil it hard or soft as your wife will permit.' The rest of the story you may imagine; the young man came home with both horses, but not an egg remained in his basket."

"That is a scandalous story, Doctor."

"True, my learned friend; but after we finish this Mumm, I will tell you another with a better moral."

Old Phrases=Continued.

"Let us," said the Doctor, "take up the familiar, every day language—the language, sir, not of the drawing room, but of the street—the language, not of the beau, but of the b'hoy, sir, and dissect it." Here the Doctor rolled up his wristbands, and armed himself with a fruit-knife, in the most formidable manner. "Let us," he continued, tapping the ringing rim of the finger-bowl, "dissect it, sir, and expose its muscles, ligaments, and tendons, its veins and its arteries, its viscera, its nerves and its ganglionic system, and sir, we will find that these old phrases are the very bones of the system, sir, the framework that sustains and supports all the rest. Yes, my learned friend, take even a tissue of slang, and you will find it full of marrow-bones!"

"Among some people the range of ideas being limited ——"

"The range of ideas being limited," interrupted the Doctor, "the range of expression is necessarily limited also. Yet, you will see how readily, even with a small stock of words, the b'hoys make themselves understood. One word passes muster for many, by dint of inflection and gesture: a single phrase sir, will often convey as many separate and opposite meanings, as a single string on Ole Bull's violin will express separate and opposite sentiments. Why, sir, the slang phrase, 'that's so,' is used to signify affirmation, confirmation, doubt, interrogation, irony, triumph, and despair; and a host besides of shades of sense relative to the subject in hand. 'You'd better believe it,' is sometimes a taunt, or a menace, as the case may be; sometimes a grave and weighty piece of advice; and sometimes significant of its own opposite—that is, 'You had better *not* believe it.' Now my learned friend, if we could only trace these phrases, and betimes we will, we· would find them to be, not the property of this generation, but the original expressions of a people very much fore-shortened in language, some centuries behind the curtain of Shakspeare; or else the result, the quotient, of some old story, from which every thing else had been subtracted."

"Doctor, pardon me for interrupting you."

"Willis," continued the Doctor, "did originate some phrases, sir, such as 'the upper ten thousand.' You see how it has been trimmed down to 'the upper ten,' and by and by it will be used to signify a class simply, without any reference to its previous purport. And in this connection the facile terminal '*dom*,' which so often has brought up the rear-guard of a sentence in the papers, is due to Willis, who struck it out in 'japonicadom'—a most happy and felicitous phrase."

·'Doctor, I would like——"

" Some authors write whole volumes without a catchword——"

"To ask if you——"

"Others again press a score of them in a——"

"Can tell me——"

"Chapter. Well, sir?"

"Whether you can tell me what was the origin of the phrase—'a fish story?,"

"Certainly," responded Dr. Bushwhacker; "every body knows that: An old Indian, who had been converted by the missionaries, got along very well as far as "Jonah and the whale,' where he faltered a little, but finally passed over that, and went on. At last he reached the history of Shadrach, Meshech, and Abednego, in the fiery furnace. 'Me no believe that,' said the Indian. 'But you must believe it,' said the missionaries. The Indian dissented; but the missionaries cleved to the point of faith at issue. At last, after a prolonged debate, in which the Indian distinguished himself by a display of natural eloquence, the old aboriginal wound up the string by saying, 'Now, I tell you, me no believe that; and since you make me mad, me no believe too *that fish story!*,"

"That is the origin of the phrase, sir, and it is not only original but aboriginal."

IX.

Art.

"My learned friend," said the Doctor, glaring at us through his critical specs, "I have seen both exhibitions, the British and the French. I was delighted sir, delighted with the French exhibition. The people of France, sir, are essentially an æsthetic people; they strive to please you sir, and they succeed in pleasing you; they rarely widen their callipers beyond the limits of decorum; they kill their tragedy heroes in abattoirs behind the scenes, and never venture to intrude upon us those coarser emotions which are independent of taste and politeness; so, sir, I visited the French exhibition with pleasure, and came away gratified. I do not remember any single pictures except those of Rosa Bonheur, and they struck me, perhaps, because they reminded me of something I had seen in nature that was familiar; but otherwise, I have only a general impression, sir, of pleasure, of great pleasure. It was far different, sir, with the British exhibition. I was not pleased with it, sir, not pleased with it. I came away, sir, with my emotions excited, and in a state of disagreement. You know my love of Shakspeare, sir! well, sir, I never felt such divine pity

for King Lear—such exquisite sympathy for Juliet (out
of the book,) as I felt when I saw those pictures of F.
Madox Brown, and Frederick Leighton. As for the bulk
of the rest, the modern school of British Art, it is expressed forcibly in a line, so contemptuous, sir, that from
my love of the æsthetic and the agreeable, I am almost
afraid to quote it. But, sir, as an arbiter of matters of
taste, I cannot refrain from saying of the modern school
of British Art : that—

'Extreme exactness is the sublime of fools,'
and, sir, you may try the measure by the spots on the
sailor boy's breeches, or the twigs on any one of the pre-
Raphaelite trees, and if you are not convinced of the
truth of the above maxim, then try it on Ruskin's own
picture, ' Study of a block of Gneiss, *Valley of Cha-
mouni, Switzerland, No.* 155.' Ruskin, sir, is a great
writer, a great rhetorician ; his persuasive powers are
wonderful, dazzling, *but not reliable, sir.* Put a pen in
his hand and Ruskin can make his mark. Put a pallet
on his thumb, and Ruskin sinks into the lowest depths
of Ruskinism."

"My dear Doctor!"

"Yes, sir, into the lowest depths of Ruskinism. His
tre-foil, cinque-foil windows are very nice things in print,
and we admire them ; as well as his lichens, mosses,
striæ, and the oxide stains of his wonderful gneiss bould-
ers ; but, sir, what is the use of having Ruskin's meagre
representation of a lichen covered, metallic stained boulder

from an obscure corner of the globe, in our parlor, when we can have the real article from the richest mineral kingdom on earth, just by rolling it in?"

"But there is the sentiment, Doctor."

"The sentiment? My learned friend, if there is no sentiment in the original, what can you look for in the mere copy?"

"But, Doctor, what do you think of Holman Hunt's Light of the World?"

"An exquisite bit of art, a happy adaptation of the school to a *single figure;* lucky was it for him that he had no other figures in the background."

"Why, Doctor?"

"Because the school has no idea of atmosphere, sir— atmosphere, distance, perspective! Look at the background figures in his picture of St. Agnes' Eve; the features, the expression of every face, painted as elaborately as if they were in the foreground. Is that the way nature exhibits her panorama? Sir, so far from features, or the expression of features, being recognizable at that distance, I can tell you that it would be difficult to say whether there were men or women, yes, bipeds or quadrupeds in that perspective."

"Nevertheless, Doctor, you must admit that they are very beautiful works of art. Just think of the man who can paint such pictures. Is he not very much elevated by genius above his fellows?"

"Unquestionably he is, and when all that is now

claimed for him has passed through the ordeal of detraction, the pre-Raphaelite, or post-Raphaelite painter, will find a proper niche, when all the symbols of his art are, to quote Shakspeare:

'In the deep bosom of the ocean buried.'

And, by the way, why not have a pre-Shakspearean school! Why not!"

"Doctor, that is a capital idea."

"My learned and dear friend, I was only in jest. A school! My dear friend, you have never yet, and never will see a *school* of great men. Intellect of the first class is great—independent—single—alone! It has no scholastic limits, no pedantry, no peers. The moment art ceases to appeal to sympathies and emotions, and contents itself with the bare representation of forms, it comes in competition with the photograph, and at once is beaten by the more elaborate delineation of the camera."

"But, Doctor, you forget the symbols of the pre-Raphaelite school!"

"Symbols, symbols! and of a school? What! has this age of intelligence to be instructed by symbols of a school of painters? If they are able to convey ideas by symbols, why do they write the names of their pictures in Saxon characters on the frames? Why not let the symbols explain the symbols? *They* teach us what art is, by symbols! Faugh! If that is high art, let me begin with the rudiments, and study it out—from the alphabet of a Chinese teacup."

X.

Accidental Resemblances.

DR. Bushwhacker came to us, to-day, in an old fashioned, full circle blue Spanish cloak, a fur cap, a carpet bag, and a small package of pemmican in his hand. He deposited these articles in the hall, shook the hand of my wife impressively, and caressed the children with warmth and tenderness. The Doctor is usually boisterous with children, but to-day he was subdued. Moreover, he gave each of them a keep-sake. To Bessy a stalactite from the grotto of Antiparos; to Lucy a little paper of sand from the Desert of Sahara; Tom had a vial of water from the pool of Bethesda; and Jack a twig of ivy from Melrose Abbey. Even the baby was not forgotten, for he had brought it a Chinese rattle, that no doubt was contemporary with the age of Confucius; and to my wife he presented a little book made of papyrus, inscribed with Coptic characters, which might have been decyphered had they not been obliterated by time. Then, putting his hand in his left vest pocket, he drew forth a present for me. It was his lancet, which, he assured me, had bled more respectable people than any other lancet in fashionable practice. "My learned friend," said he, "you have no idea of the fees which have accumulated upon the point of this instrument. But the old practice, sir, the old, venerable, respectable practice is vanishing in these new fangled, latter-day lights of science. The good old days of calomel and tartar emetic have departed. The late Surgeon General broke down the time-consecrated faith in these specifics, and now, sir, we have to study the physical idiosyncracies of a patient before we prescribe, as diligently as lawyers do when working up a case in their profession. The good old easy days are gone, sir—but I hear the dinner bell!"

The Doctor was silent during the repast. But a bottle of "Old Wanderer, 1822," as bright as a topaz, drew him out. Poising the straw stem glass between his thumb and forefinger, and viewing the shining fluid with the eye of a connoisseur, he broke forth—"My learned friend, do you suppose that the science of chemistry has advanced so far that this wine could be imitated even by a Liebig?"

"Certainly not Doctor. To any person of fine taste, all imitations must pass for imitations. They no more resemble the original than——"

"Imitations usually do. I know what you want to say, my learned friend. All plagiarisms are as inferior to originals, as copies of great pictures, or plaster casts of great sculptures, are inferior to the works which the pencil or the chisel, in the hands of a great master of his art, has accomplished. This is so well understood in the mere sensuous works of painters and sculptors that even the most accurate copy of a Raphael, or of a Leonardi di Vinci, is nothing worth comparing with the original. But how is it with literature, my learned friend ?"

" I do not understand you, Doctor."

" How is it with literature ? Do you think that you can ever build up an American literature, if the chief merit of our native authors exists only by imitation ? Dr. Drake, sir, Joseph Rodman Drake was an example. He was an original native poet, sir. Who has followed his example ? Not one."

" That would be imitation Doctor."

" No, sir. It would be *emulation*. There is a nice distinction between the two phrases."

" But what do you mean by plagiarisms Doctor ?"

" That is rather a harsh term to use. Suppose we call them 'accidental resemblances.' Now, your friend, Barry Gray, paid you a great compliment in accidentally resembling your style. My dear old friend, Washington Irving, once said to me: ' Who is this Barry Gray ? He has stolen from the Sparrowgrass Papers, the *style* of the author. Materials are everywhere, and are common property. *But a new style is the author's own.* Tell me the real name of Barry Gray, that I may know upon whom to pour the full measure of my contempt, for I hate these literary pilferers.' "

" Surely, Doctor, you know what stopped my pen at that time, and so spare me."

" Suppose we take up Halleck as an example," said the Doctor, sententiously.

"Great heavens, Doctor! Halleck! I know that 'Fanny,' has been assumed by the critics to be an imitation of Don Juan, but, really, it was written before Don Juan was published. Lord Byron's story of Beppo suggested the metre, and Halleck wrote 'Fanny' before Don Juan had crossed the Atlantic."

"What do you think," said the Doctor, "of his eulogy on Burns?

> 'And if despondency weigh down,
>   Thy spirits' fluttering pinions then,
> Despair—thy name is written on
>   The roll of common men.'"

"Well, Doctor?"

"Shakspeare, sir! Henry IV, Part I, Act III, Scene First,

> 'And all the courses of my life do show,
> I am not in the roll of common men.'"

"Ah, Doctor! Halleck intended that to be a quotation."

"Now, sir," continued the Doctor, "we have Henry (again) IV, Part I, Act IV, Scene First, as authority for another popular catch.word—

> 'There is not such a word spoken of in Scotland, as this term fear.'

And Bulwer in his Richelieu says—

> 'There is no such word as fail.'

Do you not see the palpable resemblance of these two?"

"True, Doctor, but what shall be said of them except that they are——"

"Accidental resemblances! Now, here is another example, from Paul Revere's Ride in Longfellow's Wayside Inn.

> 'Now *Soft* on the sand, now *loud* on the ledge,
> I hear the tramp of his hoof as he rides.'

But Tennyson had already written in his wonderful dramatic poem of Man—

> '*Low* on the sand, and *loud* on the stone,
> The last wheel echoes away.'

What do you think of that?"

"Ah, Doctor, you are rather hypercritical."

"Do you think so?" said the Doctor, slightly reddening, for he does not like his opinions to be impugned.

"What do you think of this from the Birds of Killingworth, in the same volume?

> 'And rivulets rejoicing, rush and leap,
> And wave their fluttering signals from the steep.' "

"Well, Doctor, I never heard that before, and it is a beautiful image."

"Beautiful! indeed it is, if one had never before read Wordsworth's ode on the Intimations of Immortality, where we have the same idea presented in a line, the rejoicing, the rush and leap of the waters, the signal note, the great concurrence of waters, in one blast, as it were—

'The cataracts blow their trumpets from the steep.'

That, sir, *is* poetry, and the other is——"

"But surely, Doctor, you must admit——"

"That Longfellow's psalm of life is original. *Ars longa vita brevis*, is cleverly rendered. As for the rest of the stanza, though I will quote the whole of it——

> Art is long, and time is fleeting, .
> And our hearts though stout and brave,
> Still like muffled drums are beating
> Funeral marches to the grave.'

I cannot quite subscribe to the originality of any part of it. In my copy of Cowley's Poems, (folio '1668,' page 13, of verses written on several occasions,) in his Ode upon Dr. Harvey, who had discovered the circulation of the blood——"

"And a great discovery it was, Doctor!"

"A great discovery, sir! As great in medical science, as Galileo's discovery of the rotation of the earth, sir. In Cowley's tribute to Dr. Harvey, we find this expression of the poet—full of his subject, the new discovery—the circulation of the blood.

> '—— the untaught heart began to beat
> The tuneful march to vital heat.'

And here we see the idea of the march, of the musical

instruments, of the band, of the drums beating, embodied in the lines of our Cambridge friend."

"So then Cowley was the originator of that thought?"

"No, sir. I did not say so. His lines had 'an accidental resemblance' to the lines of Dr. Henry King, Bishop of Chichester, who had before written in a poem called the Exequy, an ode dedicated to his deceased wife—

> 'But hark! my pulse like a soft drum
> Beats my approach, tells that I come,
> And slow, however, my marches be,
> I shall at last sit down by thee.'

There, sir, what do you think of that?"

"Why, let us all thank God, Doctor, that such things have been modernized. Who the deuce could buy Cowley or Bishop King at this time?"

"Ah, my learned friend," said the Doctor, "I do not like your remarks. I have paid a great deal of attention to these works of original men, and I would like to conserve them, apart and entire from the vulgar world."

"What good would that do, Doctor?"

Dr. Bushwhacker paused. He was evidently moving upon a different plane from the ordinary motion of mortals. His love of uncut editions floated before his eyes. Finally he broke forth:

"'The blessings of Providence, like the dews of heaven, should fall alike upon the rich and the poor.'—Andrew

4

Jackson. There, sir, you have an original quotation from one of the greatest Presidents we ever had."

"No, Doctor, for in Burton's Anatomy of Melancholy, which is one of the most comical books ever written, you will find on page 391, edition of 1836, printed for B. Blake, the following sentence:

'As the rain falls on both sorts, so are riches given to good and bad.'

That is so near Jackson's motto, that the accidental resemblance is palpable. Of course General Jackson had read Burton's Anatomy of Melancholy, my learned friend. What hadn't General Jackson read?"

"Now, Doctor, in regard to these matters, what do you think of Tennyson's
    'Flowers of all hues, and lovelier through their names,'
Introduced in the prologue to the Princess?"

The Doctor paused.—"Tennyson is certainly an original poet."

"But Milton in Book IV, verse 256, in Paradise Lost, as '*flowers of all hues.*' Do you think Tennyson stole from Milton?"

"No, that was an accidental resemblance!"

"What do you think of Lord Byron?—

    'For where the spahi's hoof has trod,
    There verdure flies the bloody sod,'

Compared with Dr. Fuller, in his Holy War, Chapter XXX.

    'Grass springeth not where the grand signior setteth his foot.'"

"Ah," said the Doctor, "you are too inquisitive, and too hypercritical. 'Grass springeth not where the grand Turk setteth his foot,' and 'where the spahi's hoof has trod, there verdure flies the bloody sod,' is the same thought expressed in different ways. One is a commonplace method of expressing a superstition common in the days of Fuller; the other a highly imaginative poetical paraphrase of Lord Byron."

"But the thought was an *accidental resemblance?* eh, Doctor?"

Dr. Bushwhacker, whose nut-pick had been busily employed during this colloquy, and who had tasted successively the Sherry, the Old Port and the Wanderer of 1822, now laid down the little steel implement, which, in his hand, looked very much like a dentist's tooth filler, brushed the lint of the napkin off his lap, and rose. "You ask me too much," he said. "You overburthen my mind with ridiculous questions, and expect me to find answers for all the quips and cranks of an erratic brain. Do you not know, sir, it is much easier to ask questions than to find answers for them? Good bye, sir; I wish you a very good day. My compliments to your good lady, who, I suppose, is asleep by this time. And a kiss for all the little ones, who, no doubt, are in the same happy condition. I am going, sir, to a country where there are no poets, nor philosophers, nor plagiarists, nor politicians. To-morrow I shall take a steamer for San Francisco, and from that place I shall go to our new

Russian American Possessions, among the Polar Bears, and the beauties of Arctic vegetation. Farewell! and perhaps you will never hear more of Dr. Bushwhacker.

———

NOTE.—After the Doctor had departed I found on my desk the following paper, which I recognized as being in his hand writing. As a literary curiosity, I have thought it worth preserving.

XI.

Sitka: Our New Acquisition.

BY DR. BUSHWHACKER.

In the Americo-Russian archipelago there is an island called by the above name, on which is the capital city of New Archangel. It is situated off a belt of land, fringed with Russian Islands, about thirty miles wide, and three hundred and forty-five miles long; which shuts off one-half of British America from the Pacific; and north of that, the great peninsula, like a shoulder of mutton, tough, sinewy and fat with Arctic animal life, rolls up into the mighty fore-arm of Mount St. Elias, and rolls down in avalanches, eternal snow-storms, glaciers, fogs, and icy rivers to the Pacific on the west side and to the Arctic Sea on the north side. To the consumptive patient the land offers few attractions, but to those philosophers, whose lungs are strong enough to endure the fatigues of a lecture-room, she has an eloquence and beauty, diversified with two volcanoes, whose throats are in a perpetual blaze of excitement. What splendor there is in yonder Aurora Borealis, that for myriads of years has played upon these lakes, streams and mountain peaks! How delicious nature is in her normal condition! I think I hear one of the Strong Minded, say to her lovely companion in philosophy! 'Ah,

Maria! let us lay aside our fans and our *chignons*, and put on snow shoes, and explore! Will you go with me from the heated atmosphere of social life into the calm sequestered retreats of Russian America? Shall we build huts of blocks of ice, like the hardy Esquimaux, and wrap ourselves in the drapery of a robe of sable skins or sea otters, worth $20,000 at least, and despise the pomp of this world? You know, my dear, sables are very cheap there. Catherine of Russia had to get her sables by keeping up a very expensive military establishment at Sitka. She was a very illustrious, strong-minded woman, to be sure; and her morals were a little loose, and she poisoned her husband; but what are those trifling enjoyments compared with carrying out a great idea? It is not so cold as the eastern side of the continent. The isothermal lines cause a great moderation in the atmosphere there. Let us establish a school there. There are 78,000 souls—if they have souls—of Calmucs, Creoles, native Indians, Kuriles, Aleutians, and Kodiaks, Kamschatkians and Esquimaux; and how pleasant it will be to teach them the rudiments! By and by they can vote. Fly with me, dear Maria! Do you not long for the snow shoes that will carry you over those vast steppes to a superior intelligence? An intelligence with nature, a communion with her visible forms, a relief from the world, and the sweet sympathy that we shall feel with the Aurora Borealis!'

The reason why the Czar wishes to dispose of this fertile territory is because he cannot conquer the North

Pole, that being the only Pole that has escaped his auto-
cratic fist. It must be said, however, that it affords us
many fine harbors for our whalers after animal petroleum,
for heretofore we have had but one decent harbor on the
Pacific coast, and that is San Francisco. Now we shall
have plenty of them, if we are lucky enough to find them
in the fogs which are perpetual there.

The principal inhabitants of this vast territory are
mountains. There is not a tree that will risk its vege-
able life by attempting to grow there; the low lands are
covered with moss instead of grass, and the best kind of
Russian shred isinglass springs spontaneously from the
crevices of the rocks. Of the amphibious animals, the
green seal or moct is most valued there, being highly
prized by the Japanese; the Muscovy duck flies about in
a very wild state in those high latitudes, while the double-
headed eagle preys alike upon the russ and the walrus.
Most of the artificial teeth in the United States are made
from the tusks of this latter animal, so that in future we
shall get our teeth free of duty. The British having heretofore had an exclusive treaty with the Russian government
to supply this place with food and ice-picks, no doubt this
lucrative branch of commerce will fall into our hands.
There is no doubt a vast quantity of gold hidden under
the soil, as it has never made its appearance above the
surface. It is proposed to get up a Russian Crushing
Company to extract this valuable ore from the veins of
Mt. St. Elias. Spruce trees not bigger than a wisp broom

grow in some patches.   These are valuable, as a beer
is brewed from them, very useful as a remedy for the
scurvy.   The castle at New Archangel is very heavily gar-
risoned with 50 Calmucs and Cossacks, mounts 24 brass-
mounted breech-loaders, five seven-pounders, twelve
horse-pistols, two mountain howitzers, one Governor, one
Russian flag, two ensigns, and a fast team of Esquimaux
dogs for flying artillery practice.   The diplomatic cor-
respondence with old Gowrowski, who is the governor of
the fort, has not been published as yet, as he asserts the
United States government cannot turn him out without the
consent of the Senate.   The vivid description of this en-
chanting country by Campbell will no doubt recur to the
reader.   Speaking of the hardy sailor on that coast, he
says :

> ' Cold on his midnight watch the breezes blow,
> From wastes that slumber *in eternal snow*,
> And waft, across the wave's tumultuous roar,
> The wolf's long howl from Oonalaska's shore.' "

XII.

Phrases and Filberts.

IT sometimes happens at the end of a dinner, when jokes and walnuts are cracked together, that the paternity of some trite quotation is put in question, and at once the wit of the whole company is set wool-gathering.

> The man who writes a single line,
> And hears it often quoted,
> Will in his life time surely shine,
> And be hereafter noted.

If every printing office had a case filled with popular phrases arranged in the manner of types, it would save much manual labor, and the compositor would be surprised to find how often he had occasion to use them. For so inextricably are these "short sentences drawn from long experience" entangled in the meshes of language, that to eliminate them would be like drawing out of a carpet, the threads that form the pattern. A few of these phrases, usually found floating in the currents of ordinary conversation, will be sufficient to consider in a paper like this: if we were to include those embraced in literature and oratory, it would require foolscap enough to cover the sands of Egypt, and an inkstand as large as one of the pyramids. Not being disposed to make such an investment in stationery at present, we shall only play the literary chiffonier and hook a few scraps from the heaps of talk we meet with every day.

Mr. John Timmins, the broker, says of that stock, "*there is a wheel within a wheel,*" without giving Paradise Lost, Young's Night Thoughts, and the Prophet Ezekiel credit for a phrase which may have saved him some thousands; and when he tells his boon companions at the club, that as for his wife, who is rather inclined to be extravagant, "*he would deny her nothing,*" he does not say how much he owes to Samson Agonistes for the words he makes use of. When he reaches his house, Mrs. Timmins takes him to task "for coming home at such an hour of the night, in such a state;" to which he replies, in a gay and festive manner: "My dear, '*To err is human—to forgive, divine,*'" from Pope's essay on criticism; to which Mrs. T. answers in a snappish way, "Timmins, '*there is a medium in all things,*'" (from Horace). Mr. T., disliking the tone in which this quotation is delivered, "*snatches a fearful joy*" (from the "Ode on a Distant Prospect of Eton College"), by saying he does not intend, in his house, to have "*the grey mare prove the better horse,*" (from Prior's epilogue). This only "*adds fuel to the flame,*" (from Milton's Samson), and Mrs. T. observes that if "*we could only see ourselves as others see us,*" (from Burns), it would be better for some people; that ever since he had joined that club "*a change had come o'er the spirit of her dream,*" (from Byron):

that when she trusted her happiness to him she had *"leaned upon a broken reed,"* (from Young's Night Thoughts III, and Isaiah 36: 6), and winds up a long lecture with the reflection that *"evil communications corrupt good manners,"* (from 1st Corinthians 15: 33). This last expression exasperates Mr. Timmins, and he asks Mrs. T., as he takes off his suspenders, " to whom she alludes ?" Is it to Perkins who had stood by him *"in evil report and good report ?"* (2d Corinthians 6: 8). Is it to Rapley? *" a man take him for all in all,"* (Hamlet, Act I, Scene Second), is *" after his own heart,"* (Acts 13: 22), and as for Badger, who had extended to him in the tight times of '36 and '37 *" the right hand of fellowship,* (Galatians 2: 9), he was as honest a man as ever breathed ; and here Mr. Timmins, with one boot in his hand and the other in the boot-jack, eloquently adds, *"an honest man is the noblest work of God !"* (from Pope's Essay). He was proud of the friendship of such men, if she meant them. Mrs. T., not at all carried away by such a flood of authorities, rather scornfully says, " O Timmins, *'what is friendship but a name ?'* " (from Goldsmith's Hermit); at which Mr. T., who by this time is undressed, and *" as mad as a March hare,"* (from the old English superstition), puts out the candle *"in the twinkling of an eye,"* (1st Corinthians 15: 52), lies down as far as possible from the *"weaker vessel,"* (1st Epistle of Peter 2: 17), courts *"tired Nature's sweet restorer, balmy sleep !"* (Young's Night Thoughts), and wakes next morning *"a sadder and a wiser man,"* (in Coleridge's Ancient Mariner).

If we turn from the frescoed bed-chamber of Mrs.
Timmins to the white-washed kitchen of Jim Skiver, the
shoemaker, we find language not less elevated. Jim
throws a leg of mutton upon the table and says: " There,
Mary, I had '*to take Hobson's choice*,'" although Jim had
neither read the 509th Spectator, nor knew that Hobson's
epitaph had been written by Milton. Jim, not "*having
the fear of*" Beaumont and Fletcher "*before his eyes*,"
(Romans 3: 18), says, if he can " catch that man wot gave
Bill Baxter a black eye the day afore his weddin' he'll
'*lamm*' him", (King and No King, Act V, Scene Third).
To which Mary replies: "I thought somethin' would
happin: '*the course of true love never did run smooth*,'"
(Midsummers Night's Dream, Act I, Scene 1), and Jim
responds, "That's so ; and they've put off the weddin'
so often that it seems kind o' '*hopin' agin' hope*,'" (Romans 4: 18). Jim thinks after they've had a "*snack*,"
(Pope and Dryden), they had better go see the Siamese
Twins ; "*twins tied by nature ; if they part, they die*,"
(Young's Night Thoughts); puts on "*a hat not much the
worse for wear*," (John Gilpin), "*dashes through thick
and thin*," (same authority and Hudibras), and after he has
seen the Siamese, requests to see the "*Lilliputian King*,"
(from Gulliver's travels).

How much language would be left us if these estrays
were returned to their lawful owners, is a question. How
could we console the dying if we had to give up to Gay's
twenty-seventh Fable the phrase, "*while there is life*

there's hope?" and what could we say to the good in misfortune if we had to restore to Prior's Ode, "*Virtue is her own reward?*" The shopkeeper who ends his long list of fancy articles with "*and other articles too tedious to mention,*" makes use of a sentence as old as the Latin language, and we would take the point from Byron's hit at Coleridge, if we were to replace in "Garrick's Epilogue on Leaving the Stage," "*a fellow-feeling makes us wondrous kind.*" So, too, must Goldsmith's Hermit lose "*man wants but little here below,*" if Young's Night Thought, IV, had its own property: and "*all the jargon of the schools,*" from Burns' 1st epistle to J. Lapraik must be rendered up to Prior's "Ode on Exodus," which has a prior claim to it. Mr. Achitophel Scapegrace thinks the biggest stockholders in the Roaring River Canal Co. will have the best chance, as "*all the big fish will eat up the little ones,*" (Pericles, Prince of Tyre, Act II, Scene First), and Mr. Bombastes Linderwold talks of a "*platform*" in precisely the same sense as Cromwell did two hundred years ago, (Queries in Letter 97, Carlyle). It is in Cromwell's seventh letter that we find for the first time that apt conjunction, "*a gentleman and a Christian,*" now somewhat threadbare from misuse, and if we want "*mother-wit,*" we must look for it in Spenser's Faërie Queen, Book IV., Canto X, verse 21. Every body has seen the man in Greek costume who sells soap by the ball but nobody but Mr. Leviticus Gaylord suggested, "that if another Greek should meet that Greek then would be a tug of war," and he has authority for saying so in the Rival Queens, Act IV, Scene First. We have to go back to Thomas ä Kempis for "*man proposes but God disposes;*" but "*what if thou withdraw and no friend takes note of thy departure?*" was written by a young man only eighteen years of age nearly fifty years ago.* If we want to look up "*the solemn brood of care,*" we can find that, "*and each one, as before, will chase his favorite phantom,*" in Thanatopsis. There, too, we will see the hills "*rock-ribbed and ancient as the sun,*" but "*old as the hills*" is older than the "*oldest inhabitant,*" and like him, has lost its parent. If we need "*to point a moral and adorn a tale,*" we must get Dr. Johnson's "Vanity of Human Wishes," and "*he that runs may read,*" in Cowper's "Tirocinium," and "*he may run that readeth it,*" in Habakuk 2: 2. If any person wish to "*consume the midnight oil,*" let him read Gay's Shepherd and Philosopher, and in Congreve's "Mourning Bride" he will find "*music hath charms to soothe a savage breast.*" "*To be in the wrong box,*" will occur to him who has dipped into the sixth book of "Fox's Martyrs," and Napoleon found "*that from the sublime to the ridiculous there is but one step,*" in Tom Paine's works translated and published in France, in 1791. We take "*buds of promise,*" from Young's "Last Day," "*and men talk only to conceal their mind,*" from his "Love of Fame," although we attribute the thought to Talleyrand. "*Good breeding*

* Bryant.

is the blossom of good sense," is not quite so familiar, but
it is also in the "Love of Fame," from whence we get
the original of what Matilda Jane Peabody believes when
she ties up her hair before the looking glass and says that
"Louisa Perkins and Betsey Baker can't hold a candle to
her." "*To hold their farthing candle to the sun*" is in
her mind, or its equivalent. "*Who shall decide when
doctors disagree ?*" is a question we may well ask between
the Allopathists and the Homœpathists, and Pope puts it
in his "Fourth Moral Essay." In "Lochiel's Warning"
we find "*coming events cast their shadows before.*" So
Tim Taffeta thinks as he sees the shade deepen upon the
brows of his creditor. So Dr. Senna thinks as he sees the
premonitory symptoms of coming apoplexy in the fair
round proportions of Alderman Broadbutton, and so
thinks Peter Pipkin as the delicate adumbration is visible
in Mrs. Pipkin's "nature's last best gift," (Paradise Lost,
Book 5, line 19), who finds herself "*as women wish to
be who love their lords*" (Douglass, Act I., Scene First),
"*not wisely, but too well.*" (Othello, Act V, Scene Last).
It is impossible to see the Ravels on the tight-rope without thinking of "*the light fantastic toe,*" and L'Allegro ;
and "*thoughts that breath and words that burn,*" live in
the magic atmosphere that surrounds the orator, as well
as in "Gray's Progress of Poesy." To make a complete
collection of these phrases would be the labor of a life ;
so numerous are they, that if the door is once opened,
they pour in "*thick as the leaves in Valambrosa,*" (Para-

dise Lost, Book I, line 303) ; and although the "*labor of love*" (Hebrews 6: 10), might entertain the scholar, yet if he were to cast these pearls before an undiscriminating multitude, after he "*had borne the burden and heat of the day,*" (Mathew 20: 12), his only recompense would be that he had made every one as wise as himself, which the true scholar cannot abide. "*Brevity is the soul of wit,*" (Hamlet, Act II, Scene Second), and we must make our discourse "*fine by degrees and beautifully less,*" (Prior's Henry and Emma). These sentences—"*jewels, five words long that on the stretched forefinger of old Time sparkle forever,*" (Tennyson's Princess), are not to be scattered with too liberal a hand, and, therefore, we shall conclude with a quotation peculiarly appropriate: "FORSAKE NOT AN OLD FRIEND: WHEN WINE IS OLD, THOU SHALT DRINK WITH PLEASURE." Eccl. 9: 10.

Does Queen Victoria Speak English?

XII.

MY friend John Common of Roscommon Bay, middle inlet, third house on the left hand side going up, where there is good anchorage for a yacht of several tons burden, propounded the above question one day, after a yawning stretch over the briny bay in a brisk breeze, followed by the usual dead calm, when in sight of home.

"Does Queen Victoria speak English?"

"Surely, John Common of Roscommon, she speaks her own *Queen's* English, and that is the *purest* language the Court of St. James has heard since the days of Edward the Confessor."

John Common of Roscommon lazily puffed his cigar under the canvass canopy of the summer sail, knocked off the ashes with the tip of his little finger, drew a fresh whiff of inspiration from his little brown deity, and said, in a soft voice of rebuke:

"I know very well that her Majesty is a pure, high-minded, pious, good woman; but my inquiry related not

to her morals, but to her language ; to her vocabulary,
if you will, which is the vocabulary of the realm ; the
court language, the language of polite society ;—in
fact, that arbitrary style of speaking which is commonly
known as the Queen's English, the mother tongue of
British scholars, statesmen, and of the highly educated
classes of that country ; and that is what I meant. I have
a theory of my own upon that subject," he continued,
" and I merely asked the question of you in order that I
might have an opportunity to answer it myself."

"A theory ! a theory !" cried out several voices from
the cabin of the yacht, where the clinking of ice had been
heard for several minutes, and out came the party. John
Littlejohn, and William Williamson, and Peter Peterson,
and Sandy Sanderson, and several others. They arranged
themselves on the seats under the shadow of the sail,
cigars were handed around ; it was a dead calm on the
bay, and so John Common of Roscommon began:

" I have never yet heard an Englishman speak, who
pretended to use the Queen's vernacular, without tracing
in his language a vein of cockney running in it, like a gold
thread through a velvet cloth. And this quite as plain
and distinct among the highly educated, as among the
rest of her Majesty's subjects.

" I maintain that custom does not sanction the misuse
of the eighth letter, or as Rare Ben Johnson quotes it,
' the queen mother of consonants,' although it may excuse
it. Certainly, when we consider the matter fairly, we

must conclude that there is as much impropriety in substituting for the beautiful Greek female name 'Helen' the modern English name of 'Ellen,' as there would be in calling 'Emma' 'Hemma,' which the Court of St. James will very speedily do, unless a stop is put to further innovation.

"In citing the name of 'Helen,' for so unquestionably the *Hellenes* pronounce it, I had a further object in view, and that was to follow up the stream of cockneyism to its classical fountain. The Greeks were probably the original cockneys—at least we can trace the *spiritus asper* and the *spiritus lenis* to them. There might have been still earlier cockneys, and it is not unreasonable to suppose that in the confusion of tongues at the destruction of the Tower of Babel, that the family of *H's* might have first adopted the unsettled and wandering mode of life which they have led elsewhere, and are now leading in the English language; but so far as that is concerned, it is mere conjecture, and, therefore, very likely to mislead us in our course of inquiry after truth."

Then he continued:

"It is quite easy to follow the current down after striking the parent spring. In the time of Romulus and Remus, no doubt the original Latin was a pure sonorous language, a little barbarous, to be sure, but stuck as full of H's as the cloves in old-fashioned boiled ham (and a rich dish that would be now, with the present tax on spices); but as the Romans waxed opulent, gave up wars and patriotism, and began to cultivate arts and lassitude, the introduction of schools prepared the way for the Greek accent; it became the rage to imitate the style of Athens, as well in its oratory as in its sculpture and in its architecture ; and when Cicero spoke in the affected and voluptuous diction of Alcibiades, and Cæsar fell at the foot of a marble image, then the decadence of Empire began.

"The languages, of which the Latin was the primitive stem, such as the Italian, the Spanish, the Portuguese and the French, easily adopted the accent of Rome when Rome was in its decay. These modern languages cast off their *H's*, and to this day the French Academy, the Spanish Academy, the Universities of Padua and of Parma have never been able to recall them. In the language of a Spanish lexicographer, 'H is not properly considered as a letter, but as a mere aspiration.' The Spanish Academy has also banished the hard sound of the h in *chimico, chimera, chamelote*, etc., by writing instead, *quimico, quimera, camelote*. So that the eighth letter is torn up root and branch, in the Kingdom of Isabella the Catholic, and the consequence is that they have a revolution in Spain every six years. In a short time Cuba will be on a detached service. It is significant that the natives of the *Siempre Fiel* pronounce 'Habana' with enough ejaculation of breath upon the first letter to blow a Spanish fleet from its anchorage.

"But to return to the Queen's English. Before the Norman Conquest England had a language of its own—

not Saxon altogether, but *English!* that great, pithy, thoughtful, bold, full-fraughted, mother tongue, which even now constitutes the substance and strength of the highest powers of intellectual expression; not to be excelled in any language. I might almost say not to be *matched* by any foreign idiom.

"I am speaking now of the pure English, that is spoken only by educated people in New York city and its immediate vicinity.

"No person who wishes to attain a lofty style can safely depart from the good old English idiom. It is to glowing eloquence and sparkling rhetoric, what a blacksmith's bellows is to a forge.

"This language, notwithstanding it was so splendidly celebrated by old Thomas Churchyard, (Tempus Henry VII), had unfortunately been corrupted long before his time by the Normans. William Conqueror introduced a court cockney dialect, which had descended from the Greek cockneys to the Roman cockneys, from the Roman cockneys to every branch of the Latin family, and from the derivatory Norman French it spread through to Whitechapel and Threadneedle streets, through Windsor and Buckingham Palaces, and from thence to the hearts and homes of an imitative people. Thus it was that the family of H's were banished from their own indigenous soil.

"That is the history of it, or chronicle, or what you will. All that I wish to say is, that we can trace the Greek taint down to the present time.

"Now, then, for examples. There is old Geoffrey Chaucer, (commonly known among the wooden spoons of Boston as Daniel Chaucer), he is full of defiled English. In the Nonnes' Priest's Tale, we have '*habundant*' for abundant; * and for hexameter he uses this outrageous substitute:

'And they ben versified commonly
Of six feet, which men clepen '*exametron.*' †

For Dante's 'Ugolino' he substitutes '*Hugelin.*' ‡ He even clips the French itself by striking an h off a French clock, and naming Horloge, '*orloge,*' § and so through all his works. Can subserviency to the ruling powers farther go?

"But every innovation has its reaction. The common people of England, in those early days, seeing that their beloved H's were being knocked off the household words, like the noses from the Elgin marbles, revenged themselves by clapping an H in front of every naked and exposed vowel. The consequence is that we have such words as '*hedge*' for edge, '*hall*' for all, '*hogshead*' for oxhead, and the like. It would be too much of a task to cite all the corruptions of a similar nature in the language. The mere mention of these will suggest swarms of others, familiar to every reader of ordinary books, to say nothing of philologists.

---

* Tyrwhitt Ed. page 129.   † Ibid, 127.   ‡ Ibid, 121.   § Ibid, 128.

"Take the word 'hedge' for example. Originally it meant something. It meant an *edge*, a boundary of shrubs, indicating the limit of the field or of the estate. We have it yet in 'box edgings,' which are partitions of garden beds, and meaning the same thing precisely. Shakspeare says, 'Upon the *edge* of yonder coppice,' etc., (Loves Labor Lost, IV, I). Now it has lost its significance in becoming a h'edge.

"So with the word '*hear*.' We speak of *hearing* an argument. That would be considered as proper Queen's English, would it not? But suppose any one should say that he had een '*h'eying*' a street fight? Would that not be a painful sound to ears polite? And yet both words are derived from their original substantives, the ear and the eye, and the verb to '*hear*' is as plain a cockneyism as the verb to heye, when we come to think of it. You say an 'ear-witness' as well as an 'eye-witness,' do you not? If anybody should say an 'hear-witness,' what would you think of that? And yet it is no greater an impropriety than 'hear' is in the mouths of polite people. No one can for a moment doubt that according to the mechanism of the language, 'to *ear*' a person is quite as proper a form of expression as 'to *eye* a person,' and that the H in 'hear' is an insupportable cockneyism. So with the superfluous 'H' in 'hall.' In old mansions in England, the main apartments, the great audience chamber, the dining-room, the vast conservatory where the noble guests sat above the salt, where the pilgrim warmed his rain-drenched, threadbare garments by the fire ; where the minstrel tuned his wretched harp, and every condition of life was represented, in this vast vault- ed chamber, the '*aula*,' the *atrium*, the all in all of the manorial and baronial residence, what right had an H to strike out the significance of the original word ? There is no doubt in this case at all. For the ' Manor All,' the ' Town All,' and so on in all the grand old English words, must be replaced. If you have a little, narrow strait be- tween your parlor and your side wall, call it an *entry*, if you will, but do not call it a h'all

" So with the bird of wisdom, the owl. Everybody has heard her note who has lived in the country. It is ' how, how, how, how, howl !' From this we get the name of this fowl of Minerva. The bird of night, in the new- born nakedness of early English, was undoubtedly the ' Howl.' We find it still in its diminutives, such as ' Howlet.'

'And keep her place as '*Howlet*' does her tower.'

In the Scotch vocabularies Houlet is the word, not *owl*. And, by the way, none of these French cockneyisms appear in either the Scottish or Irish dialects. I believe their idiomatic languages to be purer than the modern English. Shakspeare does not have any allusion to cock- neyism in his time, except when he shows his knowledge of the Greek language in his Athenian play, by putting in- to the mouth of Bottom the Weaver '*Ercles* for Hercules.*

---

* Midsummer Night's Dream, Act I, Scene Second.

"But it is needless to multiply examples. Some vacancy should be left in the mind of the listener, which he can fill up himself at leisure. Let me say here, however. that, save Chaucer, there are few writers of our earlier English who so Frenchify the mother tongue as he does. In Piers Ploughman * we have *hem* for them, and *hire* for their. In Robert of Gloster † we find 'hit' used for 'it,' as it is in the Lord's Prayer of Richard the Hermit, and so it is used to this day by some of the English, even in writing. But generally the language of these old authors was pure, as indeed it was from the time of Chaucer to the Restoration. After King Charles II came in, we had the French affectation introduced, as lively as it was in the days of William the Conqueror.

"Now a few words more: there is the word 'hatchet,' the diminutive of axe, the original of which is *eax*, Saxon, (or *ascia*, Latin). It should of course be *atchet*. So we have hatchment, a corruption of the heraldric word '*achievement*,' meaning an armorial escutcheon; then there is the word ability, which, in the dictionaries of a century old, is spelled properly, '*hability*,' or able— '*hable*,' from the French; arquebus, we say, instead of *harquebus*, and artichoke instead of *hartichoke*, and the like.

"Then, again, consider the number of words from which the H is omitted in pronunciation: 'onorable, 'um-

---

* "1362," or Circa.   † Tempus Richard II, 1174.   1208.

ble, 'umor, 'eir, 'ome, sweet 'ome, 'ow, 'onest, and the like. Then, again, such words as 'ostler for hostler, (from host or hostel), 'arbor for harbor, (a shelter), Oboe for haut bois, and so on, where the abuse is sanctioned by the dictionary makers.

"You will commonly find, too, that well-educated Englishmen (and women) say 'oo, for who, 'andiron for hand'iron, 'ow for how, and 'anging for hanging. They deny it, of course, and will, if they think they are watched, pronounce these words properly, but they are sure to relapse as soon as they are left to themselves. If you were to ask Lord John Russell, who is esteemed to be as deep in erudition as he is in diplomacy, how to spell the letter H, he would, no doubt, spell it a-i-t-c-h, when in truth it should be *h-a-i-t-c-h*, with a strong aspiration on the first letter."

CHAPTER II

"Does Queen Victoria Speak English?"

o continue," said John Common of Roscommon. "To leave this class of impediments of speech behind, and go further, we find many defects in modern English, derived from the same parentage. For example—there is no *W* in the French alphabet. If you were to ask a Frenchman to pronounce the name of the first President of the United States, he would say "Vashington," or he might, by a strong mental effort, get as near to it as *Guashington*. Just as if you were to ask him the name of the second President, he would be obliged to reply "*Hadams*," and so forth. Now there is not one single word in the English language beginning with the letter V that is not derived from the French, the Spanish, the Italian, or some of the cognate branches of the Latin family of words. There is no V in the Anglo-Saxon alphabet, none in the Mœso-Gothic, from which two tongues we derive our mother tongue, none in the earlier editions of English authors; take, for example, Grafton's or Hollinghead's Chronicles, or any other work of that

period.   Hence it is that we find such expressions in the
modern British classics as: "Now, Shiny *Villiam*, give
the gen'lem'n the ribbons," * "*vell vot* of it," † or "*vot's*
the use of giving *vay* so long as you're 'appy;" of which
forms of expression numbers could be produced if one
could give his mind, his time, and his attention to it.   I
do not mean to say that the substitution of the V for the
W is common to the upper classes of Great Britain.   Far
from it; but I do mean to say that this innovation is
creeping up, and will, by and by, beget a class of words
foreign to the genius of the English tongue, just as the
dropping of the H has produced such words as ostler and
arbor.

In confirmation of this, let me state that a distinguished
traveler and philosopher, Mr. George Gibbs, of Long
Island, after a residence of a quarter of a century on the
Northwest coast of this continent, has written a dictionary
of the Chinook jargon, or Trade Language of Oregon, prepared for the Smithsonian Institute, Washington, D. C.,‡
in which he shows conclusively that the Chinook, the
Nootkan, the Yakama, the Cathlasco, (which is a corrupted form of the Watlala or Upper Chinook), the
Toquat (which he spells Tokwaht), and the Nittinak languages have been corrupted by the mis-pronunciation of
the English of the Hudson's Bay Company.   The consequence is, that there is scarcely an H in its proper place

---

* Pickwick Club, Ed. 1836, Vol. I, p. 95.
† The Golden Farmer, a play, in three acts; author unknown, 1835.
‡ Ed. 1863, 8vo. p. 44.

in any of the dialects of the Northwestern tribes of the Pacific, and W's are substituted for V's to such an extent, that in his dictionary not one word beginning with the latter consonant can be discovered. It is, however, a consolation to know that these are the most prominent innovations in those rich and beautiful occidental tongues. After complaining that the Spanish and French voyageurs have left traces of their languages in the earlier Chinook, he says:

"It might have been expected, from the number of Sandwich Islanders introduced by the Hudson's Bay Company, that the Kanaka element would have found its way into the language, but their utterance *is so foreign to an Indian ear, that not a word has been adopted.*" *

If this be so, we can imagine what a highly respectable tone prevails in Kanaka society of Queen Emma.

But to return. The substitution of the French "*V*" for the English "*W*" led to the retaliatory process, by which every free born Englishman makes all things hequal. Just in proportion to the cockneyism of the upper classes in the middle ages arose the defiant attitude of the cockneyism of the lower classes. The doubleyous began to crowd into the lower ten million vocabulary. "*W*eal pie" took the place of the other word:

> "Even the tailors 'gan to brag,
> And embroidered on their flag,
> 'AUT WINCERE AUT MORI.'" †

---

* Thackeray's Ballads, Ed. 1856, p. 121.
† Gibbs' Dictionary of the Chinook Jargon, Ed. 1863, p. viii, (Preface).

There was a stout battle between the starveling French
V and the broad bottomed English W, and to this day it
has continued. There is not a member of any English
legation in any part of the world, at this present time,
who dares to spell "Vaterloo" with a V. And this is in
obedience to the dictates of the lower, and, I might
almost say, the illiterate classes ; for after all, a mob has
a great deal to do with fixing the expression as well as
the meaning of words.

Since I am so far committed to this subject, I must
continue a little longer ; but let me say here, that if I tax
the old nation from which we are derived, with speaking
a very impure language, let me at least have the credit
of doing so in a friendly spirit. Let us with one hand
soothe the American Lexicographical Eagle, while with
the other we smooth the bristling mane of the British
Polyglot.

In further confirmation of what I have already advanced,
permit me to recall to every mind another phrase of the
language of the realm, in order to prove that the queen
speaks broken French. I do not mean to say that she
does so intentionally, for surely no one can have a higher
regard for that good lady than I have. In fact, we are
both of an age ; both born on the same day of the same
month in the same year, perhaps in the same hour, if
degrees of longitude could be computed with accuracy,
(of different parentage, I admit). What I mean to say
is, that she speaks imperfect English, both of herself and

through her ministers, through her parliaments, through her lords and her lord mayors, through her ladies and her laundresses, through her British museum, and her Billingsgate market. After all this explanation, which might lead to a digression, let me return to the point that I intended to make when I said that the queen speaks broken French.

Nothing is more striking to an American when he first visits London than the constant misuse of the French "*A*" pronounced *aw* by the high school of cockneys. The lower classes of her majesty's subjects use the plain old fashioned English "*A*" as an expletive, as well as an offset to the other (a fashion, by the way, derived from the Greeks, for their language is full of expletives), in this manner—I was "*a-going*," or, I was "a-thinking," or, I was "a-'oping," or, I was "a-hironing," and so on through the whole family of verbs. Now this misuse of the vowel is so common to the common people, that to hear it from the lips of any person is sufficient to suggest that his education has been quite imperfect. This being so, *is it quite fair* that we should acquit Lord Brobdignag of a similar charge, when we hear him read from a master of style, thus: "They say-*aw* that it was *aw*-Liston's firm belief, that he-aw was aw-great and neglected tragic actaw. They say-aw that ev-aw-ry one of us believes, in his heart, or would like-aw to have others believe, that he-aw is something which he is aw-not!"

It is very true, as Dr. Samuel Johnson says in his little

article on Orpiment, that "talk is elastic." But even talk
he mis-spells, (for he means "*talc*," a mineral), nevertheless we will accept the mistake as being truer than his
definition in every way. Talk is elastic! but what shall
be said of the petrifiers of the living words of our language? What shall we say, for example, of the abuses
of Webster's Dictionary? When an elastic language
becomes a concretion of fossils—when its life has gone
out, and lexicographers have left nothing of it but its
organic remains—what should be done with them? To
compel them to speak plain English would be impossible,
for that they do not comprehend. What should be done
with them? Surely the Cadmus teeth they sow should
rise up and reap them.

I suppose, in time, that the good old English word
"Beef-eater," as applied to those broad-backed warders
of the Tower of London, will degenerate into "*Buffetier*"
(French), as now a revolution is being effected in a similar word—and "*cur*," which some writers claim as a
Hindoo word, "*Ischur.*" * Blackstone, (a famous law
writer of the last century), has endeavored to elevate the
tone of the British bar by changing the honest old name
of "bum-bailey" in this wise: He says "that the special
bailiffs are usually bound in a bond for the due execution
of their office, and thence are called 'bound-bailiffs,'

---

* Dictionary of Cant and Slang. London. Ed. 1860, p. 11.

which the common people have corrupted into a *much more homely appellation, burn-bailey !*" *

I cannot here avoid expressing my regret that a very creditable weekly paper in the British booksellers' interest in London should have its classical name corrupted into "a much more homely appellation." I mention this the more cheerfully from the fact that it has always abused American authors, and, therefore, when I say that I regret it, you will understand that it is an act of generosity on my part. I allude to the *Athenæum*, which has never recovered from the punishment that Bulwer inflicted upon it when he called it the "Ass-i-neum," a name by which it has been known to cultivated people in all parts of the world, from the days of Paul Clifford down to this time.

But these corruptions of the language we must frown down. Let us take a bold stand against other cockney-isms creeping into public use, such as "*cab*" for cabriolet, "*pants*" for pantaloons, "*canter*" from the Canterbury pilgrimages at the good old-fashioned ambling pace, and the like; for, if we do not, the age of progress will make the word "gentleman" a dead language, and only its cockney substitute, the "*gent*," will be known in dictionaries and newspapers.

A few more words and I shall wind up my squid.

There is a slang phrase of Parisian-French, which I

---

* Blackstone's Commentaries on the Laws of England. 4to. Oxford, 1766. Book I., Chap. IX., p. 346

cannot recall at this moment, that expresses a peculiar way of shortening words, and running one into another, in use among the fashionable people of the continental metropolis, so that it is very difficult for a novice to understand their aristocratic *argot*.

This shrinkage, this corrugation, this wrinkling up of words, so that a good long sentence which should be sonorous and expressive, becomes as shrivelled as a washerwoman's thumb, is beautifully implanted in the modern English. Go to the House of Lords and hear the debate between Lord Brobdignag and the Marquis of Lilliput! Only by the skill of the practised reporter can that tongued and grooved dialect be interpreted. I shall not give you a sentence by way of example, but only a few specimen bricks of this modern Babel.

It is well known that in the glorious old English tongue every word carries a meaning with it; a little history in its womb, such as those beautiful phrases "belly-timber," as applied to food, and "bread-basket," as applied to its receptacle. So the lord of thousands of broad acres in Merrie England—

"Lovely in England's *fadeless* green."—*Halleck*—

was called the Earl of "*Beau-champs*," from the Norman French, as in Scotland the name of Campbell is derived from an Italian origin meaning the same thing, as Beauchamps, "Campo-bello." Just as the constellation in the Southern hemisphere called "Charles' Oak," recalls the

history of that royal and ragged refugee, in Boscobell, so
a vast number of words in English once represented ideas.
They were words with poetry and history locked up within
them, like flies, in perpetual amber. The river "Alne"
in Cumberland, the stream celebrated in many a border
foray, has upon its banks the ancient town of Alnecester,
and the "home of the Percy's high-born race," Alnwick
Castle. Should you inquire for either place, there is not
a man in England who would understand you. But just
ask for Anster and Annick, and there is not a red-coated
boot-brushing boy in the neighborhood of Temple Bar
that cannot tell you where to find the train that will carry
you to the residence of the Lord's of Northumberland. I
remember once that I hired a post and pair to go down to
Stratford-upon-Avon. A jaunty postilion in spotless, white
dimity knee breeches, white top boots, silver-rimmed hat-
band, and a whole carillon of bell buttons on his jacket,
touched his hat as I stepped into the "shay." "Drive me
round," said I, "by the way of Charlecote Hall!" for I
wished to see the place where Shakspeare was tried for
deer-stealing. That was a puzzler. The friendly landlord
of the "Warwick Arms," the aged Pensioner of the Bear
and Ragged Staff; the obsequious waiter; the radical
tailor, who made red riding coats for fox-hunting squires
and d——d them in the bitterness of his sartorial soul;
the small boy that always followed a stranger as the mite-
fly follows a cheese; the parochial Beadle with his bell;
the blue eyes of the chambermaid, from an upper story

of the Warwick Arms; all, in dire suspense, in that dewy morning, waited to hear the reply of the post-boy. There was no reply. Presently an underhostler, who had been hovering around the horses like a spiritual gad-fly, whose wings were horse-brush, and curry-comb, spoke out in a foggy voice: "P'raps the gemman means Chawcut?" Shade of Shakspeare! And *chawcut* it was, as everybody understood it there. So it is that in this puckered-up English,—Warwick, itself a splendidly significant name, becomes Waric. The Beauchamp Chapel is Beecham. Charlesbury has lost its ancient significance in Chawbree. Cholmondely is Chumlee. Berwick of old renown, "*royal* Berwick's beach of sand," is now Berric; Candle-wick Street in London, is Cannick; Gloucester is Gloster, Smithfield is Smiffld, and Worcester—Wooster! So, too, that word dear to every domestic tie, "housewife," is "*hussif*," subtle is "*suttle*," and High Holburn, *I-oburn*.

Can anybody doubt that the corruption of these good old expressive English words into bastard French is not undermining the Queen's English?

And the mis-spelling of these and many other words will soon follow the mis-pronunciation, as, indeed, some do now—witness "Gloster!" I once hired an English hackman to take me from a once-celebrated hotel in New York to a once-celebrated Hudson river steamboat. It chanced that when we reached the wharf the boat was casting off, and the driver called out to me, " You 'ad better 'urry up, sir, or she'll be h'off, and you can pay me

the fare when you get 'ome agin." So when I did get
back again, and asked for my little account, he referred
to his pocket remembrancer—"Mr. C., June 14th, 1842.
m. o. to *e. u.*" "What does that mean?" "'Merican
'Otel to 'Endrick 'Udson, sir!"

"And what," said little Tweedle, "are we to do. If
we go to England, are we to fly in the face of every man
there? are we to insist upon our own pronunciation, and
endeavor to find out famous localities by naming them in
the language used in the Saxon Heptarchy?"

"Certainly," said John Common of Roscommon, "I
would advise you to agitate this subject; to call things by
their right names in that benighted kingdom; to inquire
for places that nobody can tell you anything about, so
that you can teach the ignorant natives what should be the
names of their choicest, their dearest, their most cherished
localities. You can do this thing, for you have a genius
for disturbing the old herring-bone foundations of ancient
edifices. And I will give you all the glory of being the
pioneer, if you choose to take this matter of reform of
the tongue upon your own shoulders. I may adopt it
also. But I shall not trumpet forth my claims upon the
world until I find that you have succeeded. I think I
feel a fresh breeze creeping up. Haul away on the jib
halyards! Let us see if we can't work up the creek.
The champagne has been in the cooler over there for five
hours now and the meats only go to the brander upon
signal. So haul up the dinner signal! Ah, here comes
the breeze! Up sails, and now to dinner."

XIV.

The Noses of Eminent Men.

OF all the quadrupeds, the elephant is, unquestionably, the most sagacious. And, although some have fondly imagined that his sagacity is wholly owing to his great bulk—just as we are apt to think wisdom is peculiar to the fat, or judgment to the thickset—yet, in justice to the elephant, we must not allow the world to repose upon so absurd and preposterous an error. If mere bulk were wisdom, what shall be said of the hippopotamus; of coroners, and aldermen; of justices to the peace, the rhinoceros, and the commissioners of the Patent-office; of prize-medal pigs, and Gen.—? We see, at once, the fallacy of the popular belief, when we consider the very opposite relations existing between bulk and wisdom, in the above examples. It is needless here to enter into an elaborate detail of the sympathetic attachments of the brain and the nose, extending through an infinite ramification of nerves, arteries, ganglions, and tissues, nor of the power of the organ itself to express emotion; to scorn, to sneer, to snivel, to affirm, or deny; to put itself intrusively where it is not wanted; to be arrogant, haughty, conceited: to suffer indignities; to be a sleeping-trumpet, and a moral, psalm-singing instrument in the conventicle. The relations between the brain and this organ, are, therefore, nearly equivalent to those between a ship and its rudder—with the trifling difference, that we are guided by one, and led by the other. These facts being established, all that is required to be known further, is, whether the dimensions of a nose being given, it is possible to arrive at a fair estimate of the subsidiary mental power, if not, indeed, at a regular scale, such as Kepler has laid down with regard to the planetary system. To this we answer in the affirmative. Let us take the wisest of brutes as an instance. The height of the tallest elephant in the jungles of Africa is ten feet and a half, and the length of his proboscis, from the lower suture of the coronal bone (*os frontis*), to the tip, is exactly seven feet and an inch. Now, if we add to the height of the elephant his weight and circumference, we find the proportion of the organ to the sum total to be exactly 19 11-60 per centum. If we take, as an offset to this, the commonest and most familiar zoological example, viz., the proportions existing between the weight, height, and bulk of the hippopotamus, and the length of his nose, we find them expressed in round numbers by the fractions 132-33900. And it is a curious scientific fact, that the mental capacities of the two animals—I mean the power of mind—the "think" that is in them, when carefully measured, exhibit nearly the same figures. If, then, guided by these astonishing results, we take up any plethoric body of men— say the United States Congress, or the State Legislature,

for instance—it is very easy to determine precisely their
intellectual value, in a psychological point of view. The
average of a board of aldermen, reduced to the scale of
half an inch to the foot, exhibits so near an approxima-
tion to the proportions of the lesser animal, that we might
call them the " city hippopotami", and be accurate enough
for ordinary purposes. On the other hand, if we attend
a meeting of strong-minded women, we find a prodigious
development of this feature. Strong-minded women have
immense noses, with some flat hats and a variety of spectacles. Jews, also, are singularly gifted; but we make allowance of at least one-third for organs of this pattern, on
account of the natural hook, from the eyebrows to the tip.
We once had the honor of being intimate with one of the
most profound scholars and thinkers in Holland, who was
so long-nosed and near-sighted that he wiped out with his
nose half of what he wrote with his pen—thereby show-
ing a memorable instance of wisdom. The average
length of a fully-developed, intellectual, male nose, is
precisely two inches and a half from the indention between the eyes to the extreme end of the cartilage.
Washington's nose was 2 5-8 inches; but the presidential
average has, so far, been what we have stated above—
Jefferson, for example, representing the longs, and Fill-
more the shorts. Wellington and Napoleon differ only
the sixteenth of an inch, both being above the average;
Lord Brougham, who is an encyclopædia of general information, follows a feature three inches in length! the
average nose of the Century Club is 2 9-16; Thackeray's

nose is 2 5-8—precisely the length of the nose of the "Father of his country;" President Johnson's is 2 9-16; Irving's, 2 7-12; Bryant's, 2 6-11; Dickens's, 2 3-8; Durand's, 2 7-13; Gen. Scott's, 2 5-10; Longfellow's, 2 6-11; Gen. Sherman's 2 1-2; Macaulay's, 2 5-9; Farragut's, 2 3-4; Commodore Wise's, 1 7-12; Tennyson's, 2 4-7; Hoffman's, 2 7-13; the average magazine nose of this city is 1 5-8; in Philadelphia, 1 7-8; McClellan's is 2 8-12; Verplancks', 2 5-8; Bayard Taylor's, 2 6-11; we shall have Fredrika Bremer's by next steamer; the nose of the Academy of Design, 2 5-9; Browning's, 2 5-9; Miss Mulock has a very respectable feature for a woman, being 2 1-4; Jean Ingelow, 2 1-8; Bonner's, 2 1-2; Seward's, nearly 3 inches, and our own a snub.

In making our measurements, we have had the greatest difficulties to encounter, by reason of the foolish desire of many to be represented as measuring more than they are entitled to. But, as we know by experience how often scientific data are put aside as worthy of no credit, because of a few trifling defects or errors, we have been guided only by our instruments. We know it is very hard to refuse a sixteenth of an inch, when it is asked by a friend, as a particular favor, but, nevertheless, our "reflections" must be accurate and reliable, or else they will be justly condemned. In pursuance of our theory, we have engaged Mr. Pike, the eminent mathematical instrument maker, to construct for us a noseometer, of the greatest capacity, and will, from time to time, furnish our readers with the results of the observations taken therewith.

XIV.

(From the Bunkum Flagstaff and Independent Echo.)

𝔅unkum 𝔐useum.

Just opened, with 100,000 Curiosities, and performance in Lecter Room; among which may be found

TWO LIVE BOAR CONSTRICTERS,

Mail and Femail.

ALSO!!

A STRIPED ALGEBRA, STUFT.

BESIDES!!

A PAIR OF SHUTTLE COCKS
AND ONE SHUTTLE HEN—alive!

THE!

SWORD WHICH GEN. WELLINGTON FIT WITH
AT THE BATTEL OF WATERLOO! whom is

six feet long and broad in proportion.

WITH!!!

A ENORMOUS RATTLETAIL SNAKE—a regular

whopper!

AND!
THE TUSHES OF A HIPPOTENUSE!
Together with!
A FINGAL TIGER: AND A SPOTTED LEPROSY!
Besides
THE GREAT MORAL SPECTACLE OF "MOUNT VESUVIUS."

PART ONE.

Seen opens. Distant Moon. View of Bey of Napels. A thin smoke rises. *It is the Beginning of the Eruction!* The Napels folks begin to travel. Yaller fire, follered by silent thunder. Awful consternation. *Suthin rumbles!* It is the Mounting preparin' to Expectorate! They call upon the Fire Department. *It's no use!* Flight of stool-pidgeons. A cloud of impenetrable smoke hang over the fated city, through witch the Naplers are seen makin' tracks. Awful explosion of bulbs, kurbs, torniquets, pin weels, serpentiles, and terrapins! The Moulting Laver begins to squash out!

End of Part One.

COMIC SONG.

The Parochial Beedle..................Mr. Mullet.

LIVE INJUN ON THE SLACK WIRE.

Live Injun..........................Mr. Mullet.

OBLIGATIONS ON THE CORNUCOPIA, BY SIGNOR VERMICELLI.

Signor Vermicelli.....................Mr. Mullet.

In the course of the evening will be an exhibishun of
Exileratin' Gas! upon a Laffin Highena!

Laffin Highena........................Mr. Mullet.

PART TWO.

Bey of. Napels voluminated by Gondola Lites. The lava
gushes down. Through the smoke is seen the city in a
state of conflagration. The last family! "*Whar is our
parents?*" A red hot stone of eleving tuns weight falls
onto 'em. The bearheaded father falls scentless before
the statoo of the Virgin! *Denumong!!*

The hole to conclude with a

GRAND SHAKSPEARING PYROLIGNEOUS
DISPLAY OF FIREWURX!!

Maroon Bulbs, changing to a spiral weel, witch changes
to the Star of our Union: after, to butiful p'ints of red
lites; to finish with busting into

A BRILLIANT PERSPIRATION!

During the performance a No. of Popular Airs will be
performed on the Scotch Fiddle and Bag-pipes, by a real
Highlander.

Real Highlander..........................Mr. Mullet

Any boy making a muss, will be injected to once't.

As the Museum is Temperance, no drinkin' aloud, but
anyone will find the best of lickers in the Sloon below.

XV.

𝔘𝔭 𝔱𝔥𝔢 ℜ𝔥𝔦𝔫𝔢.

A LEAF FROM A NEW BOOK.

HE clouds now began to break away—once more we see the distant peaks of the Siebengebirge and the castled crag of Drachenfels—a flush of warm sunlight illuminates the wet deck of the Schnelfahrt; the passengers peep out of the companion-way, and finally emerge boldly, to inhale the fresh air and inspect the beauties of the Rhine. As for the Miller of Zurich, he had taken the shower as kindly as a duck, shaking the drops from his grey woolly coat, as they fell, and tossing off green glass after green glass of Liebfraunmilch, or Assmanshauser, from either bottle. Betimes his pretty wife joined us, and walked on tip-toe over the wet spots; the sun came out, hotter and hotter; the deck, the little tables, the wooden seats, began to smoke; overcoats came off, shawls were laid aside; plates piled up with

sweet grapes and monstrous pears, green glasses, and tall
flasks of Rhine wine, were handed around to the ladies,
and distributed on the tables; and the red-cheeked German boy whose imitations of English had so amused us,
shouted the captain's orders to the engineer below, in a
more cheery voice—' *Slore! backor! forror!* ' "

I had 'had an indistinct vision of a pair of whiskers at
the far end of the breakfast table, brushed out *à l'Ang-
laise* in parallel lines, as thin as a gilder's camel's hair
brush. These whiskers now came up on deck, attached
to a very insignificant countenance, a check cap, and a
woollen suit of purplish cloth, such as travellers from
Angleterre enjoy scenery in. Across the right breast of
this person, a narrow black strap of patent leather wound
its way until it found a green leather satchel, just across
his left hip; while over his left breast, a similar strap
again wound around him, and finally attached itself to a
gigantic opera glass in a black leather case. All these
implements of travel, with little else to note, paced
solemnly up and down the now dry deck of the Schnelfahrt.

In the meantime, my glass, map, guide book, were all
in action, castle following castle, Rolandseck, Rheineck,
Andernach, and all the glorious panorama, rolling in view
with every turn of the steamer. And chiefly I enjoyed
the conversation of my Miller of Zurich, whose plump
forefinger anticipated the distant towers and battlements
which he had seen so often, for so many times, in yearly

trips upon the river. Nor was I alone, for from every stand-point of the deck were fingers pointed, and glasses raised, at the glories of the castellated Rhine.

But in the midst of this excitement and enthusiasm, that purple traveller, with whiskers and straps, satchel and opera glass, walked up and down, unobservant of the scenery, miserable and melancholic, without a glance at the vineyards, or the mountains, or the castles. Then I knew that he was an Englishman, doing the Rhine.

He walked up to our table, where old Zurich and his pretty wife were seated before the grapes and the wine, where my shawl and satchel were flung—map spread, and guide-book open—and said, in that peculiar English voice which always suggests catarrh—

"Going up the Rhine, sir?"

"*Rather*," said I, drily, (for I hate bores).

"Aw!"—now the reader must translate for himself—

"Forst time ye' beene h'yar?"

"Yes," I answered, "is it your first visit also?"

"Aw—no! 'beene hea-r pu'foh; sev-wal taimes. How fawr 'goin, sawr?" (Don't talk of Yankee inquisitiveness).

"To Mayence, and no further this evening." (Opera glass levelled directly at Ehrenbreitstein).

"Gaw'ng to Hydl'bug?"

"I·think so."

"Hydl'bug's 'good bisness, do it up in 'couple of awhrs."

Here old Zurich makes a remark, and says:

"Military engineers build, that other military engineers may destroy."

MYSELF.—"Are those yellow lines against the hill masonry ?—parapets ?"

OLD ZURICH.—"Fortified from top to bottom."

"Gaw'ng to Italy?" chimes in the camel's hair whiskers.

"No," (decidedly no).

"Gaw'ng to Sowth 'f Fwance ?"

"Probably."

"Wal, if 'r not gaw'n t' Italy, and you'r gaw'n to South 'f Fwance—gaw'n to Nim ?"

"*To Nismes ?* what for ?"

"'F yawr not gaw'n to Rhawm, it's good bisness to go to Nim—they've got a ring thar."

"A ring ?"

"Yas, 'ont ye knaw ?"

"A ring ?"

"Yas—saim's they got at Rhaome; good bisness that—do it up in tow hawrs; early Christians, y' knaw, and wild beasts !"

"Oh, you mean the Roman amphitheatre at Nismes—a sort of miniature Coliseum."

"Yaas, Col's'm."

"No, sir, I am not going to Nismes"—another look at Ehrenbreitstein and its shattered wall.

"Never be'n up th' Rhine before," quoth whiskers.

" No,"—we are approaching the banks of the "Blue Moselle."

" Eh'nbreitstine's good bisness, and that sort o' thing —do't in about two hawrs!"

" I do not intend to stop at Ehrenbreitstein, and, therefore, intend to make the best use of my time to see the general features of the fortress from the river."

"Aw—then y'd better stop at Coblanz, and go t' Wisbad'n, by th' rail."

" What for ?"

" Why, the Rhine, you know, 's a tiresome bisness, and by goin' to Wisbawd'n from Coblanz, by land, you escape all that sort aw-thing."

" But I do not wish to escape all this sort of thing— I want to see the Rhine."

"Aw!"—with some expression of surprise. " Going to Switz'land ?"

" Yes."

" Y' got *Moy* for Switz'land ?"

"Moy ? I beg your pardon."

" Yes, Moy—Moy; got Moy for Switz'land ?"

" Moy—do you mean money ? I hope so."

" Ged Gad, sir, no ! I say Moy."

" Upon my word, I *do not* comprehend you."

" Moy, sir, Moy!" rapping vehemently on the red cover of my guide book that lay upon the table. "I say Moy for Switz'land."

" Oh, you mean *Murray.*"

" Certainly, sir, didn't I say Moy ?"

XVI

The First Oyster-Eater.

THE impenetrable veil of antiquity hangs over the antediluvian oyster, but the geological finger-post points to the testifying fossil. We might, in pursuing this subject, sail upon the broad pinions of conjecture into the remote, or flutter with lighter wings in the regions of fable, but it is unnecessary: the mysterious pages of Nature are ever opening freshly around us, and in her stony volumes, amid the calcareous strata, we behold the precious mollusc—the *primeval bivalve,*

————"rock-ribbed! and ancient as the sun."—BRYANT.

Yet, of its early history we know nothing. Etymology throws but little light upon the matter. In vain have we carried our researches into the vernacular of the maritime Phœnicians, or sought it amid the fragments of Chaldean and Assyrian lore. To no purpose have we analyzed the roots of the comprehensive Hebrew, or lost ourselves in the baffling labyrinths of the oriental Sanscrit. The history of the ancient oyster is written in *no* language, except in the universal idiom of the secondary

strata! Nor is this surprising in a philosophical point of
view. Setting aside the pre-Adamites, and taking Adam
as the first *name-giver*, when we *reflect* that Adam lived
IN-land, and therefore never saw the succulent periphery
in its native mud, we may deduce this reasonable conclusion : viz., that as he never saw it, he probably never
NAMED it—never!—not even to his most intimate friends.
Such being the case, we must seek for information in a
later and more enlightened age. And here let me take
occasion to remark, that oysters and intelligence are
nearer allied than many persons imagine. The relations
between Physiology and Psychology are beginning to be
better understood. A man might be scintillant with
facetiousness over a plump "Shrewsbery," who would
make a very sorry figure over a bowl of water-gruel.
The gentle, indolent Brahmin, the illiterate Laplander,
the ferocious Libyan, the mercurial Frenchman, and the
stolid (I beg your pardon), the *stalwart* Englishman, are not
more various in their mental capacities than in their table
æsthetics. And even in this century, we see that wit
and oysters come in together with September, and wit
and oysters go out together in May—a circumstance not
without its weight, and peculiarly pertinent to the subject-
matter. With this brief but not irrelevant digression, I
will proceed. We have "*Ostreum*" from the Latins,
"*Oester*" from the Saxons, "*Auster*" from the Teutons,
"*Ostra*" from the Spaniards, and "*Huitre*" from the
French—words evidently of common origin—threads spun

from the same distaff!   And here our archæology narrows
to a point, and this point is the pearl we are in search of :
viz., the genesis of this most excellent fish.

"Words evidently derived from a common origin."
What origin ?   Let us examine the venerable page of history.   Where is the first mention made of oysters ?   Hudibras says :

> ————"the Emperor Caligula,
> Who triumphed o'er the British seas,
> Took crabs and ' OYSTERS' prisoners (mark that!)
> And lobsters, 'stead of cuirassiers;
> Engaged his legions in fierce bustles,
> With periwinkles, prawns, and muscles,
> And led his troops with furious gallops,
> To charge whole regiments of scallops,
> Not, like their ancient way of war,
> To wait on his triumphal car,
> But when he went to dine or sup,
> More bravely ate his captives up;
> Leaving all war by his example,
> Reduced—to vict'ling of a camp well."

This is the first mention in the classics of oysters ; and
we now approach the cynosure of our inquiry.   From this
we infer that oysters came originally from Britain.   The
word is unquestionably *primitive*.   The broad open
vowelly sound is, beyond a doubt, the *primal*, sponta-
neous thought that found utterance when the soft,
seductive mollusc first exposed its white bosom in its
pearly shell to the enraptured gaze of aboriginal man !
Is there a question about it ?   Does not every one know,

when he sees an oyster, that *that is its name?* And hence we reason that it originated in Britain, was latinized by the Romans, replevined by the Saxons, corrupted by the Teutons, and finally barbecued by the French. Oh, philological ladder by which we mount upward, until we emerge beneath the clear vertical light of Truth!! Methinks I see the FIRST OYSTER-EATER! A brawny, naked savage, with his wild hair matted over his wild eyes, a zodiac of fiery stars tattooed across his muscular breast—unclad, unsandalled, hirsute and hungry —he breaks through the underwoods that margin the beach, and stands alone upon the sea-shore, with nothing in one hand but his unsuccessful boar-spear, and nothing in the other but his fist. There he beholds a splendid panorama! The west all aglow; the conscious waves blushing as the warm sun sinks to their embraces; the blue sea on his left; the interminable forest on his right; and the creamy sea-sand curving in delicate tracery between. A *Picture* and a *Child* of Nature! Delightedly he plunges in the foam, and swims to the bald crown of a rock that uplifts itself above the waves. Seating himself he gazes upon the calm expanse beyond, and swings his legs against the moss that spins its filmy tendrils in the brine. Suddenly he utters a cry; springs up; the blood streams from his foot. With barbarous fury he tears up masses of sea moss, and with it clustering families of testacea. Dashing them down upon the rock, he perceives a liquor exuding from the fragments; he sees the white pulpy delicate morsel half hidden in the cracked shell, and instinctively reaching upward, his hand finds his mouth, and amidst a savage, triumphant deglutition, he murmurs—OYSTER!! Champing in his uncouth fashion bits of shell and sea-weed, with uncontrollable pleasure he masters this mystery of a new sensation, and not until the gray veil of night is drawn over the distant waters, does he leave the rock, covered with the trophies of his victory.

We date from this epoch the *maritime* history of England. Ere long, the reedy cabins of her aborigines clustered upon the banks of beautiful inlets, and overspread her long lines of level beaches; or penciled with delicate wreaths of smoke the savage aspect of her rocky coasts. The sword was beaten into the oyster-knife, and the spear into oyster rakes. Commerce spread her white wings along the shores of happy Albion, and man emerged at once into civilization from a nomadic state. From this people arose the mighty nation of Ostrogoths; from the Ostraphagi of Ancient Britain came the custom of Ostracism—that is, sending political delinquents to that place where they can get no more oysters.

There is a strange fatality attending all discoverers. Our Briton saw a mighty change come over his country— a change beyond the reach of memory or speculation.— Neighboring tribes, formerly hostile, were now linked together in bonds of amity. A sylvan, warlike people had become a peaceful, piscivorous community; and he himself, once the lowest of his race, was now elevated above the *dreams* of his ambition. He stood alone upon the sea-shore, looking toward the rock, which, years ago, had been his stepping-stone to power, and a desire to revisit it came over him. He stands now upon it. The season, the hour, the westerly sky, remind him of former times. He sits and meditates. Suddenly a flush of pleasure overspreads his countenance; for there just below the flood, he sees a gigantic bivalve—alone—with mouth agape, as if yawning with very weariness at the solitude in which it found itself. What I am about to describe may be untrue. But I believe it. I have heard of the waggish propensities of oysters. I have known them, from mere humor, to clap suddenly upon a rat's tail at night; and, what with the squeaking and the clatter, we verily thought the devil had broken loose in the cellar. Moreover, I am told upon another occasion, when a demijohn of brandy had burst, a large " Blue-pointer " was found, lying in a little pool of liquor, just drunk enough to be careless of consequences—opening and shutting his shells with a " devil-may-care " air, as if he didn't value anybody a brass farthing, but was going to be as *noisy* as he possibly could.

But to return. When our Briton saw the oyster in this defenseless attitude, he knelt down, and gradually reaching his arm toward it, he suddenly thrust his fingers in the aperture, and the oyster closed upon them with a spasmodic snap! In vain the Briton tugged and roared;.

he might as well have tried to uproot the solid rock as to move *that* oyster! In vain he called upon his heathen gods—Gog and Magog—elder than Woden and Thor; and with huge, uncouth, druidical oaths consigned all shell-fish to Nidhogg, Hela, and the submarines. Bivalve held on with "a will." It was nuts for him certainly. Here was a great, lubberly, chuckle-headed fellow, the destroyer of his tribe, with his fingers in chancery, and the *tide rising!* A fellow who had thought, like ancient Pistol, to make the world his oyster, and here was the oyster making a world of him. Strange mutation! The poor Briton raised his eyes: there were the huts of his people; he could even distinguish his own, with its slender spiral of smoke; they were probably preparing a roast for him; how he detested *a roast!* Then a thought of his wife, his little ones awaiting him, tugged at his heart. The waters rose around him. He struggled, screamed in his anguish; but the remorseless winds dispersed the sounds, and ere the evening moon arose and flung her white radiance upon the placid waves, the last billow had rolled over the FIRST OYSTER-EATER!

I purpose at some future time to show the relation existing between wit and oysters. It is true that Chaucer (a poet of considerable promise in the Fourteenth Century) has alluded to the oyster in rather a disrespectful manner; and the learned Du Bartas (following the elder Pliny) hath accused this modest bivalve of "being incontinent," a charge wholly without foundation, for there is

not a more chaste and innocent fish in the world. But
the rest of our poets have redeemed it from foul aspersions
in numberless passages, among which we find Shakspeare's happy allusion to

"Rich *honesty* dwelling in a POOR house."

And no one now, I presume, will pretend to deny, that
it hath been always held

"Great in mouths of wisest censure!"

In addition to a chapter on wit and oysters, I also may
make a short digression touching cockles and lobsters.

A Literary Curiosity.*

MACAULAY in the Exordium to his History, proposed to bring his narrative down "to a period within the memory of men still living." The phrase was doubtless chosen for its ambiguity; so as to *in*clude or to *ex*clude some notice of our Revolution. If the following extracts be genuine (and for their authenticity I do not vouch), they favor the former hypothesis. They purport to be sketches for a future volume: stone, rough hewn, for an edifice which, alas! the master did not live to complete.   HISTORICUS.

CHARACTER OF WASHINGTON.

"The post of Commander-in-Chief of the insurgent armies was of vital importance. Yet, the man who, of all men, was fitted to fill such a post adequately was at hand. The Congress knew it; and with a unanimity that rarely marked their proceedings, selected George Washington—a delegate from Virginia. The reader will naturally pause at the mention of a name which is regarded with fond idolatry by a federation of great commonwealths; which History has admitted into the company of founders of empire with Romulus and Gustavus,

*See Preface.

and into the roll of great captains with Hannibal and
Frederic : and which is pronounced with equal veneration
on the banks of the Thames and on the banks of the
Ganges. Both the circumstances of his birth and the
circumstances of his education had fitted him for the part
he was called on to play. In his blood, of English origin,
there was blended something of the fiery valor of the
cavaliers of Rupert, with something of the resolute energy
of the soldiers of Oliver. His form, in its matchless union
of vigor and grace, had foiled the pencil of Stuart and the
chisel of Chantry. He had known the salutary discipline
of early toil. With his stipend of a guinea a day as a
surveyor, he had acquired, in youth, the art of controlling
himself. In manhood, by the exercise of patriarchal
dominion over thousands of acres and hundreds of slaves,
he had acquired the art of controlling others. Equally
fortunate had been his public career. He had served in
the armies of the Crown, and against the natives of the
wilderness. He had thus learned something, both of des-
ultory and of disciplined warfare. At a later day, and
on a wider theatre, his knowledge of the one enabled him
to surprise the Hessians at Trenton ; and his knowledge
of the other to entangle Cornwallis in the toils of York-
town.

"His courage was of the truest temper. Stoic savages
told with wonder how he alone was calm when the soldiers of Braddock were slaughtered like sheep ; and Continental veterans loved to narrate how his face shone with

heroic fire as he rallied the broken battalions at Monmouth. His intellect was solid and comprehensive. The natural ardor of his temperament was subdued by a judgment of singular accuracy and prudence. His unaffected piety showed itself alike on public and on private occasions: when he drew his sword at Cambridge: when he sheathed it at Annapolis: when he knelt alone in the snowy solitudes of Valley Forge.

"And, indeed, all the strength of his intellect, and all the resources of his character, were needed for the task he had undertaken. For he had undertaken to confront the finest infantry of Europe with an army of tradesmen and farmers—half clad, half fed, and wholly undisciplined. In the ranks, the spirit of patriotic ardor was but too often allied with the spirit of turbulent freedom. At the council board, there were officers to whom the precedence of a colleague was more galling than the tyranny of the common oppressor. He had to deal with deliberative bodies that acted when they should have debated, and with executive bodies that debated when they should have acted; with an army that murmured at his activity, and with a government that blamed his inaction; and he was forced to exhibit, to both government and army, at one time the reckless courage of Charles XII, and at another time the serene patience of Marlborough.

"Nor must his claims to civic wisdom be passed unnoticed. His style, founded, it is true, on the turgid masterpieces of that period, was accurate and comprehensive.

IIis talent for abstract speculation was not contemptible. He presided with commanding wisdom over that assemblage of wise and ingenious statesmen, who framed a system of government in imitation of a great system, in which the centrifugal force of the separate Commonwealths and the centripetal force of the Federal authority were balanced with consummate skill. Nor did he exhibit less wisdom when called on to put in motion the machine which he had helped to frame. He resisted the unjust rule of many men, as he had resisted the unjust rule of one man ; and saw with prophetic eye the issues of that insane freedom that ended in the ' carmagnole ' and the ' guillotine.' Nor was the calm splendor of his setting unworthy of the long day of glory. He beat his spear into a pruning hook ; and planted choice trees, and reared rare breeds of animals with the same conscientious energy, with which he had ruled armies and governed cabinets.

"And yet, the truth is that characters of such perfection excite neither the just, sympathy nor the just admiration of the great mass of mankind. The very foibles of irregular greatness are a bond of sympathy and a source of interest. Most readers will turn away from a ruler who was never unjust, and from a general who never swore, to follow the amiable amours of IIenry IV, or the picturesque passion of IIildebrand. So, also, do the defects of imperfect natures serve to render, by the force of contrast, their merits more striking. The eloquence

of Tully stands out in flaming characters against the
dark background of that timorous nature ; and the glance
of Bacon, the philosopher, seems more comprehensive when
we compare it with the glance of Bacon, the venal judge,
lowered obliquely on a bribe.   The mental eye is misled,
as the physical eye is misled by the ruins of Palmyra or
the Cathedral of Cologne.   The imagination outstrips the
reality, and bestows an unmerited grandeur on the restored
temple and the completed church.   But the harmonious
adjustment of the mental and moral faculties of Washington, prevent us, at the first glance, from duly estimat-
ing the extent of those faculties.   We are like the
traveller who stands for the first time in that splendid
structure which the genius of Michael Angelo has reared
for the Catholic hierarchy.   He cannot at once justly estimate the length of that endless nave, or the expanse of
that awful dome.   And not until he discovers, by repeated observation, that the baldaquin which covers the
altar is as lofty as a palace, and that the cupids that flit
about the door are as big as giants, will he feel assured
that he treads the floor of the largest building on the
earth."

The Character of Franklin.

.   "The new ambassador was Benjamin Franklin, one of
the foremost citizens of the young Republic, and one of
the foremost citizens of the older republic of science.   He
was of humble origin.   Both in Boston, the place of his

birth, and in Philadelphia, the place of his adoption, he had wrought at that art, 'preservative of all arts,' of which the followers, like ships that bear spices and odors from the East, retain something of the precious cargoes they are employed to distribute. The clearness of his intellect was equalled by the clearness of his perceptions. Under the name of Poor Richard, and through the humble medium of an 'Almanac,' he put forth a system of homely ethics, in which the virtues of temperance, probity and industry were explained and commended in aphorisms of ingenious terseness. Nor did he fail to practice what he preached. He was speedily honored with offices of trust, both from the Colonies and the Crown. And when differences, that sprang partly from criminal interference and partly from criminal neglect, arose between the two countries, he exerted himself strenuously, first to prevent, and then to remove those differences. The hour for reconciliation passed away: and he now stood up for war with the same placid courage with which he had stood out for peace. He was one of the Committee that drafted the great Declaration. He was now sent to represent the good cause at the Court of France, and at the bar of European opinion. An extraordinary reception awaited him. He was widely and justly known as an eminent man of science—as the Columbus of electrical discovery. The French nation is, beyond all other nations, fond of striking effect and picturesque contrast. And nothing could be more stri-

king or picturesque than the spectacle now presented. A
Quaker diplomatist was about to appear in the most
artificial of courts: a new Archimedes was to come from
the land of the Natchez and the Mohawk: the legate of
the latest republic was to recall the image of antique
wisdom and of antique virture—of the Grecian Solon and
the Roman Regulus. Haughty courtiers bent in emotion
before him: brilliant beauties struggled for a kiss; sculptors and painters pursued him with merciless assiduity;
the Academy rang with applause when Turgot's adulatory
Latin described the sage as one 'who had wrested the
thunder from heaven and the sceptre from tyrants:' and
upon a ship of war, that was sent on its mission of death
and destruction under the desperate Paul Jones, was
bestowed, with pardonable inconsistency, the name of
'Poor Richard.'

"The chief glory of Franklin lies in this—that he was
the greatest of the pupils of Bacon. And, indeed, he
was such a pupil as Bacon would have delighted to honor.
To both pupil and master, philosophy was not the mystic
goddess of Plato, or the impracticable vixen of the school-
men. She was an angel of beneficence and a minister of
mercy; an Elizabeth Fry or Florence Nightingale. Her
mission was to relieve human suffering and to advance
man's estate. And, in truth, Franklin's long and successful career was a triumphant application of these
principles. No sooner had the electric spark glided down
the kite-string than the lightning-rod was invented for its

innocuous descent. The maxims of Poor Richard were devised not only for the household of the Quaker mechanic and the dealings of the Quaker tradesman, but for the government of States and the intercouse of nations. Even the barren tactics of chess were made to furnish lessons for the higher warfare of life. Nor did his philosophy fail to bear her fruits to the philosopher himself. The virtues of self-respect and self-reliance that walked by his side, when he entered Philadelphia with a loaf of bread under his arm, did not desert him when he listened, amid the frowns of hostile statesmen, to the pitiless sarcasm of Weddeburne; nor when he stood, the centre of universal homage, in the brilliant court of Louis.

"Zealous theologians have attacked the orthodoxy of his creed; casuists have cavilled at the imperfection of his ethics. But he was doubtless a good man; he was surely a great man. And he richly deserves the title of 'the most useful of the children of men'—a title which Franklin himself would have prized beyond all the gifts of fortune nd all the laurels of fame."

The Race Between the Hare and the Hedgehog, on the Little Heath by Buxtehude.*

FROM THE LOW GERMAN OF SCHRODER.

THIS story is a tough one to tell, youngsters, but true it is for all that! for my grandfather, from whom I have it, used always to say, when he told it: "True must it be, my son, otherwise one could not tell it so at all!" And this is the way the story ran:

'Twas on a pleasant Sunday morning, toward harvest time, just as the buckwheat blossomed. The sun had gone brightly up into the heaven; the morning wind swept warm over the stubble; the larks sang in the air; the bees hummed in the buckwheat; the good folk went in Sunday gear to church, and all creatures were happy, and the hedgehog also.

The hedgehog stood before his door with his arms folded, peeped out into the morning air, and chirruped a little song to himself, just as good and just as bad as a hedgehog is wont to sing on a pleasant Sunday morning. And as he was singing to himself, in a cheery little voice,

---

* See Preface.

all at once it came into his head he might just as well,
while his wife was washing and dressing the children,
take a little walk into the field to see how his turnips were
standing.   Now the turnips were close to his house, and
he used to eat them with his family, so that he looked
upon them as his own.   No sooner said than done.   The
hedgehog shut the house-door to after him, and took his
way to the field.   He had not gone very far from the
house, and was about to turn, just by the thorn bush which
stands there before the field, near the turnip patch, when
he met the hare, who had gone out on a similar business,
namely, to look after his cabbages.   When the hedgehog
caught sight of the hare, he bid him a friendly "good
morning!"   But the hare, who, in his own way, was a
mighty fine gentleman, and held his head very high,
answered nothing to the hedgehog's greeting, but said to
the hedgehog, putting on thereby a most scornful mien:

"How happens it, then, that thou art strolling about
here in the field so early in the morning?"

"I'm taking a walk," said the hedgehog.

"Taking a walk?" laughed the hare, "methinks thou
mightest use those legs of thine for better things."

This answer vexed the hedgehog hugely, for he could
stand almost anything, but his legs he did not like to
have spoken about, because they were crooked by nature.

"Thou thinkest, perhaps," said the hedgehog to the
hare, "thou could'st do more with thine own legs!"

"That's what I do think," said the hare.

"That depends upon the trial," quoth the hedgehog. "I bet that if we run a race together, I beat thee hollow!"

"That's quite laughable, thou with thy crooked legs," said the hare, "but I've nothing against it if thou art so bent upon it. What's the bet?"

"A golden louis d'or and a bottle of brandy!" said the hedgehog.

"Done," said the hare, "fall in, and then it may come off at once."

"Nay, there's no such hurry," said the hedgehog, "I'm still quite hungry; I'll go home and get a bit of breakfast first; within half an hour I'll be here again on the spot."

With this the hedgehog went his way, for the hare was also content.

On the way the hedgehog thought to himself:

"The hare trusts to his long legs, but I'll fetch him for all that; he's a fine gentleman to be sure, but still he's only a stupid fellow, and pay he shall!"

Now when the hedgehog came to his house, he said to his wife: "Wife, dress thyself in my gear, quickly, thou must go with me to the field."

"What's all this about?" said his wife.

"I've bet the hare a golden louis d'or and a bottle of brandy that I beat him in a race, and thou must be by."

"O my husband!" began the hedgehog's wife to cry, "art thou foolish? hast thou then quite lost thine understanding? How canst thou wish to run a race with the hare?"

"Hold thy mouth, wife," said the hedgehog, "that's my business; don't meddle with men's affairs. March! dress thyself in my clothes, and then come along."

What could the hedgehog's wife do? She had to follow whether she would or no. When they were on the way together, the hedgehog said to his wife: "Now listen to what I have to say. See'st thou, on the long acre yonder will we run our races. The hare runs in one furrow and I in another, and we begin to run from up there. Now thou hast nothing else to do than to take thy place here in the furrow, and when the hare comes up on the other side thou must call out to him: "I'm here already!" With this they had reached the field; the hedgehog showed his wife her place and went up the furrow. When he got to the upper end the hare was already there.

"Can we start?" said the hare.

' Yes, indeed!" said the hedgehog.

"To it then!" and with that each placed himself in his furrow, and the hare counted one, two, three! and away he went like a storm wind down the field. But the hedgehog ran about three steps, and then ducked down in the furrow and sat still.

When the hare, on the full bound, came to the lower end of the field, the hedgehog's wife, called out to him. "I'm here already!" The hare started and wondered not a little; he thought not otherwise than that it was the hedgehog himself that ran out to meet him: for, as every one knows, the hedgehog's wife looks just like her husband.

But the hare thought: there's something wrong about all this! Another race! At it again! And away he went again like a storm wind, so that his ears lay flat on his head. But the hedgehog's wife staid quietly in her place. When the hare came to the upper end the hedgehog called out to him, "I'm here already." But the hare, beside himself with rage, cried: "Another race! at it again!"

"I'm quite willing," answered the hedgehog, "just as often as thou likest."

So the hare ran thee and seventy times, and the hedgehog held out to the very end with him. Every time the hare came either below or above, the hedgehog or his wife said "I'm here already!"

But the four and seventieth time the hare came no more to the end. In the middle of the field he fell to the earth and lay dead upon the spot.

So the hedgehog took the louis d'or and the bottle of brandy he had won, called his wife out of the furrow, and both went home together: and if they have not died, they are living still. So happened it that on the Buxtehude heath the hedgehog ran the hare to death, and since that time no hare has ever dreamed of running a race with a Buxtehude hedgehog.

But the moral of this story is, first; that no one, however high and mighty he may think himself, shall let it

happen to him to make merry over an humble man, even
if he be a hedgehog; and secondly, that it is advisable,
when one marries, that he take a wife out of his own
condition, and who looks just like himself. He, therefore
that is a hedgehog, must look to it that his wife is also a
hedgehog; and so forth.

XVIII.

What is the Cause of Thunder?

A SERIES of observations, and a single experiment, would throw some light upon this important question. Take, for instance, a summer afternoon when the air is close and sultry, and the atmosphere rarefied, when respiration is laborious, and no wind stirring among the leaves. But, on the distant horizon, there are indications of vapor; not rolling clouds, but thin exhalations from the earth, drawn up by the heat of the sun. Suddenly this humid veil is illuminated by flashes, and people call it heat lightning, summer lightning, sheet lightning. I wish particularly to direct attention to the fact, that this exhibition of electricity is not often accompanied with other phenomena peculiar to thunder storms. No rain follows the flash, nor is any report heard ; and, furthermore, these illuminated vapors are always *much elevated.*

It is idle to say that on account of distance from the earth the report is not audible; for few persons, familiar with mountain heights, can fail to remember that some

time or other they were *in the midst of such an atmosphere*, when the lightning appeared to surround them,
apparently within a few feet of them, flashing on every
side, yet without rain or detonation. In this condition
the atmosphere is said to be highly charged with electricity. But surely we cannot accept this as equivalent to
the same meaning applied to a Leyden jar, fresh from
contact with the knob of the electric machine. Indeed,
is not the *contrary* very possible? Would not the data
show that, in such a condition the atmosphere, instead
of being highly charged, had not its usual percentage of
electric stimulus? Experiments with the electrometer
might prove this supposition to be correct, and, on the
other hand, it might prove it to be incorrect. But one
thing cannot be disproved nor denied—that air, highly
rarefied by heat, and *humid*, is air, plus water; and also
that in this condition air is susceptible of being silently
illuminated by electricity. This point being settled, we
will proceed to the next—which is, "What is the cause
of Thunder?"

The learned, down to the latest moment of going to
press, have advanced no further than this, that "thunder
is a noise produced by THE EXPLOSION OF LIGHTNING, or
by the passage of lightning from one cloud to another! or
from a cloud to the ground." Whoever has read the celebrated treatise of John Conrad Francis de Hatzfield
upon the subject, will find a far more plausible theory
advanced by that sagacious philosopher, and quite as

amusing as the modern idea, that the sound of thunder is analogous to the snap produced by holding the knuckle of one's forefinger to the brass bulb of an electrical machine!—an explanation that has never satisfied any reasonable mind. Let us see if there be not a rational solution of the mystery.

The phenomena of thunder storms are: first, heavy clouds; then lightning; then the report, and then a *fall of rain!* Now, let us trace the consequence to its source. The rain is produced by two causes, either sudden condensation of watery vapors or clouds, by colder temperature, or *the formation* of water by the action of the electric fluid. The first explains itself; the latter is linked with the subject of this paper. Let us, therefore, confine ourselves to that rain only which follows the thunder. Rain water is composed of two elements, oxygen and hydrogen. Hydrogen is a combustible gas, and oxygen supports combustion. A stream of pure hydrogen, ejected from a pipe into pure oxygen, burns brightly in perfect silence. But, mixed with oxygen, it explodes upon taking fire; just as a young man, having his own fortune to make, goes quietly to work until he gets a partner with a tremendous capital. The relative aspects of silent lightning and noisy lightning may be compared by a simple apparatus sold at any chemists; it is a tin lamp filled with inflammatory gas. So long as the gas is allowed to burn in small quantities it is taciturn, but, exposed to a larger mixture of oxygen, it goes off with a loud report. This is a lamp that any spark of electricity can ignite. And then again the product of the flame is water! The union of hydrogen and oxygen is water. What meteoric phenomenon is so simple as this, that thunder is caused by the electric spark uniting with rare-fied air plus oxygen, and rarefied vapor plus hydrogen, detonating, recompounding, and forming rain!

XIX

A French Breakfast.*

MLE Prince de Talleyrand gave a *déjeûner à la fourchette* at which the illustrious Brillat Savarin was a guest. This great philosopher gives us the bill of fare, interspersed with his own reflections and directions, which I have translated for the edification of all *gourmets*.

Yours,   P. D.

1st. Guinea hen's eggs fried in quail's fat, spread with a coulis (gravy) of écrevisse (a species of crawfish), very warm, each egg being a single morsel, and taken at a mouthful, after having been well turned in the coulis.

Eat pianissimo.

After each egg drink two fingers of old Madeira. This wine to be drunk with reflection. (*Recueillement*).

2d. Lake Trout with Montpelier butter, iced (butter made with aromatic herbs). Roll each morsel nicely and perfectly in this high-flavored seasoning.

Eat allegro.

Drink two glasses of fine Sauterne or Latour Blanche. To be drunk contemplatively.

---

* See Preface.

3d. Fillets of the breast of Grouse, with white truffles of Piemant—raw, in slices.

Place each fillet between two layers of truffles, and let them soak well in gravy *á la périgueux*, made of black truffles served apart.

Eat forte, on account of the white truffles being raw.

Drink two glasses of Château Margaux; the beautiful flavor of this wine will be most apparent after drinking.

4th. Roasted Rail on a Crust, *a lá Sardanapale ;* the legs and side-bones to be eaten only; the leg not to be cut in two; take it between the thumb and fingers; salt it lightly; put the thigh part between the teeth and chew it all, meat and bone.

Eat largo and fortissimo, at the same time take a cut of the hot crust, prepared with a condiment of liver and brain of woodcock, goose liver of Strasbourg, marrow of red deer, and pounded anchovies, highly spiced.

Drink two glasses of Clos Vougeot; pour out this wine with emotion, and drink with a religious sentiment.

5th. Morilles (a species of large and exquisite mushrooms), with fine herbs and essence of ham; let these divine cryptogamas melt in the mouth.

Eat pianissimo,

Drink a glass of Côte Rôtie, or a glass of very old Johannesberger. No recommendation as to the way of drinking this wine (the Côte Rôtie); it is commanding and self-imposing; as to the Johannesberger, treat it like a venerable patriarch.

6th. Bouchées à la Duchesse, with pine-apple jelly. Eat amoroso.

Drink two or three glasses of Champagne, Sillery Sec, Verzeney, non Mousseux (still) iced to snow.

7th. Brie Cheese, or Estanville (near Meaux).

Drink one glass of Port.

Then, if you please, an excellent cigar (demi regalia de Cabañas), after which one small glass of Curaçao, and a siesta, during which you will dream of the beauties of the dinner to come.

Each course of such a breakfast must be served only at the time the cook is ready; the guest must wait, not the cook, so that the dishes may be presented in perfect order.

XX.

Dainty Hints for Epicurean Smokers.*

HOEVER has been in Havana must needs recollect the little brazier, with its ball of white ashes, beneath which a live hard-wood coal, called a "*candela*," glows all day for the accommodation of smokers in every house. This we thought once a dainty device. But our friend, Master Karl, has given us some new, delicate and fragrant suggestions:—

"It is an established canon that the purest and most elevated *tastes* or flavors are unmixed—simple. I respectfully submit that in smoking tobacco, this rule by no means holds good.

And here I might cite the learned *Winstruphius* who in his 'Epigrammata,' puns so learnedly on Bacchus and To-Bacco, and their mutual flavoring influence. This I spare you. Likewise the lucubrations of *Schioppius Dunderhedius*, who in speaking most horrifically, *De odore fetida tobacci*, distinctly analyzes it into two smells—one infernal, the other diabolical. This spared also, (by request).

* See Preface.

"But I mean simply to say that a *point* may be given to a good cigar by lighting it from wood—not from the timber of a lucifer match, but from a smoldering, smoking fragment of a log, either hickory, oak, or even pine. And note ye, good fellows all, that the earlier in the season this is done, the more delicate is the *goût;* yea, this rule holds so far good, that on the first crisp evenings in September, no musk-rose or violet that is—nay, no vitivert—nay, no ess bouquet—nay, no florimel, nay, no eau de cypre—nay, no hediosmya—nay, no daintily-ambered *aqua coloniæ* or any Paradisaical sweets that be, can surpass the *odorat* of the first whiff of a wood-lighted cigar.

"Yea, and more. If you smoke light, and mild, and dry, preferring Latikéa and Knaster to fine-cut, tumback and chopped cavendish, there is a class of perfumes—that I ween, which Piesse places as the third note in the gamut of good smells—a certain spicy oriental class, such as cascarrilla, or a faint admixture of santal, which perfumes the axe which lays it low, which in no wise detracts from piping joys. And I tell you in all truth, that Virginia leaf, with these sweet delights, and with sumach or kinni kinnick therein gently mingled, spreads around such a pastilled, ecclesiastical cathedral air, blended with dim souvenirs of the rue Bréda, that he who smokes thereof is oftentimes in tone to sing the high song of King Solomon, or the lyrics of the Persian land, wherein love and devotion are so curiously entwined, that no sensation that is, can be compared thereto, unless it be the kissing of your sweetheart during sermon-time under the lee of a high-backed old-fashioned pew.

> " ' Ita dixit ille Rector
> Er wollt's nicht anders han,
> Vale semper bone Lector,
> Lug du und stoss dich dran
> *Gut Gesell ist Rinckman*.' "

10

XXI.

𝔚𝔞𝔰 ℭ𝔥𝔞𝔪𝔭𝔞𝔤𝔫𝔢 𝔎𝔫𝔬𝔴𝔫 𝔱𝔬 𝔱𝔥𝔢 𝔄𝔫𝔠𝔦𝔢𝔫𝔱𝔰?*

NEW YORK, July 1st, 1867.

THE author of the following two communications, written seven years ago, in now revising them, finds melancholy thoughts taking the place of the gay and festive feelings in which they were originally composed. In those seven years of civil strife which brought sorrow to the hearts of thousands, whose loved ones, whose "beautiful and brave," fell in the battle-field, death did not spare some of the best and noblest of those who were sportively mentioned in these papers.

Dr. Francis has passed away—Dr. Francis the jovial, the kind-hearted, the man of boundless curiosity and unerring memory, of large and sound acquirements, the genuine and enthusiastic New Yorker, who has preserved the choicest memorials of the men of the last generation in that city to which he himself so long gladdened and instructed.

President Felton, of Harvard University, is no more. New York, still mourns the death of one of her most eminent surgeons, Dr. John Watson.

The memory of all men of professional excellence, however high it may have been, is proverbially brief.

> "Feeble tradition is their memory's guard."

* See Preface.

Thus the fame of the distinguished skill of Watson must soon fade away, like that of Kissam, of Wright, of Post, and even within a few years that of Mott. But the memory of Dr. Watson will be preserved by his volume on "The Medical Profession in Ancient Times," a book equally agreeable and impressive, very learned, yet very original. That memory will also be preserved and cherished among a limited but very select class of students, in law, in medicine and in intellectual science, by his elaborate, acute and exhaustive printed opinions as a medical expert; in the great, the genial, the liberal, the wise, the accomplished scholar, one of whose Homeric criticisms is specially combated in these papers, who is there described as a person of the highest scholarship, armed with the authority, and clothed with the dignity of Jupiter, he, too, was soon suddenly snatched away from the station he adorned, and the studies which he loved.

To those honored names must I add that of Thackeray. He was one well known familiarly in our American cities, and there are still hundreds who quote his criticisms on our "Big Bursts of Oysters," as well as on our old Maderia, so plentiful and so prized but twenty years ago, while the portraits of Col. Newcome, of Becky Sharpe, and many more, remain, life-like in the minds of thousands.

But such recollections will touch and sadden only some few of my older readers. The passages relating to the lamented dead, have been therefore left unaltered, in the wish to give to such of any younger generation who may casually look into this book, a passing glance at the pursuits and opinions of some of the noted literary men among us in 1860.

——— ———, August 7, 1866.

MY DEAR COZZENS:—I had hoped to spend my vacation in quiet idleness, with a rigorous and religious abstinence from pen and ink. But I cannot refuse to comply with the request you urge so eloquently, placing your claim to my assistance not only on the ground of old friendship, but also as involving important objects, literary and scientific, as well as social and commercial; all of them (to repeat your phrase and Bacon's), "coming home to the business and bosoms of men."

You desire me to inform you, after careful examination of all the authorities, "whether the ancient Greeks or Romans, during the classic ages, were acquainted with champagne."

In such an inquiry, at once scientific and classical, it is all-important that the question should be stated with logical precision. Bacon himself has taught us that the judicious statement of the question (*prudens interrogatio*) is one half the way to scientific discovery.

Now, I may safely presume that you do not mean to ask whether the territory of Champagne was known to the ancients. Any Freshman can tell you that the fair land on each side of the murmuring Marne, and up the vine-clad sides of the mountains, was part of ancient Gaul, known and subject to the Romans, and designated as part of different provinces at different periods of the Roman sway.

On this point and all relating to it you can get whatever information you desire from Cluverius and D'Anville, or the Fathers of Trevoux. But this, I take it, you cannot mean, though it is the literal sense of your request.

Nor, in my judgment, can you mean to ask, whether the Greeks and Romans were acquainted with the wines of the growth of that part of old Gaul which, under the ancient regime of France, was called the province of Champagne. Of course the Roman colonists in Gaul knew and used the wines therein grown and made; but from the account given by the elder Pliny, of the wines there produced, they bore little resemblance to the present wines of Champagne, whether *mousseux crémant*, or still. They are not named with any respect in Pliny's statement of the one hundred and ninety-five (195!) sorts of wine which in his day were counted fit for the Roman market, of which only eighty kinds were admitted to be " wines of authority for good tables"—" quibus auctoritas fuerit mensâ," as he says, unless I misquote him. The art of wine-making was then in its very infancy in Gaul. Indeed, it was not until the days of the great and good Ingulphus, the Seventeenth mitred Abbot of Verzeney, who was also Dean of Rheims—(I give that great man the titles by which he was known in the last forty years of his life, although his most admirable and important inventions and improvements in the making and management of wines were made whilst he was still only curé of Verzy on the mountains, and afterwards Archdeacon of Ay, in the low country along the Marne)—I say, that it was not until the days of the aforesaid Ingulphus (*supradicti Reverendissimi* Ingulphi as the *Rheims Chronicle* styles him), that the wines of Campagne attracted the attention of Royalty. Soon after that they became the constant accompaniments, *de rigueur*, of all "good men's feasts." I write, as you know, out of reach of my own library, as well as of that of our university, and must trust altogether to memory. Otherwise I could not resist the temptation of expatiating further in the praise of this great benefactor of humanity. I will only add that the great Ingulphus of whom I speak, and to whom we all owe such an *impayable* debt of gratitude, was the one of the Rohan family, and must not be confounded with the three other very able and distinguished men of the Latinized name of Ingulphus, or Ingulphius, (for the name is spelled both ways), who figure in public affairs in the twelfth and thirteenth centuries.

The great Ingulphus prosecuted his vinous experiments and effected his discoveries during the reign of the famous Philip Augustus; or rather, Philip Augustus reigned in France during his time, which, by a very noteworthy coincidence, was the very period when, according to the best Irish antiquaries their Milesian forefathers discovered and perfected the manufacture of whisky, *usky*, or *the* water, as it was called in the ancient tongue of the Emerald Isle; though in the cognate dialect of the Scotch Gaelic, it was known as *uisgee*. These epochs also corresponded with the date when Magna Charta, the palladium of England's liberty, was wrung by the English from their reluctant monarch. No sound philosopher can suppose that coincidences like these are accidental. No, no:

"There are more things in heaven and earth, Horatio,
    Than are dreamt of in your philosophy."

But, to return to your inquiry. Having, by the process of philosophical elimination, excluded much vagueness and danger of error, I proceed to reduce your inquiry to the shape of the *prudent interrogation*, the logically exact questioning, of the school of Bacon and Newton. Your inquiry, then, must be this. Did the ancients, in the high and palmy days of their eloquence, philosophy and poetry, either in Greece or Rome, or in both, know and use (and of course become fond of) any effervescent wine or wines having the chemical qualities, as carbonic acid gas, with the tartarous and saccharine constituents, the physiological and dietetic qualities, *aroma*, *bouquet*, etc., together with those other properties either belonging to the science of the laboratory or to that of the table, which have been so beautifully stated by my good friend Dr. Mülder, Professor of Dietetic Chemistry in the University of Utrecht, in his "Chemistry of Wines," as being essential to the true wines of *Champagne*, whether mousseux or *demi-mousseux?*

In this statement of the question, you see, I purposely exclude the *vin non-mousseux*, or what is less philosophically expressed in English by the name of "*still* Champagne." This I do because in the vulgar and popular use, such wines are not included under the term Champagne, although grown and made in that District, and some of them, as Sillery, of the very highest merit, gastronomic and dietetic, convivial, social, and moral, and especially in those qualities which the physiology of the table designates as *Oxyporian*.

Thus, I think that the preliminary question is clearly settled with an Aristotelian precision, such as the learned gentlemen who discuss questions of Contagion and Infection in academies and conventions would do well to imitate. I then proceed to the investigation itself. This I am not ashamed to affirm that I do with perfect confidence in the successful result; for I do it, not like my learned friends just mentioned.

> "Cæca regens filo vestigia."

Or, as it is translated in my new version of Virgil, (now on the press of Ticknor & Fields)—

> "With stumbling steps along the dubious maze,
>   Tracing with half-seen thread the darksome ways."

But with a bold and firm step, lifting high the blazing torch of classic lore, which pours its floods of light forward in my path.

The conclusion to which I come is simply that the Greek and Roman gentlemen and scholars, in the high and palmy state of their literature and art, had used and enjoyed wines similar to the effervescent, foaming, sparkling, or creaming wines of Champagne.

I have stated the precise question, and the conclusion to which my mind has logically arrived.

It would be descending not a little from the dignity of learning to recapitulate any of the steps by which that conclusion was attained, and the various authorities on which it rests.

It is a wise general rule never to give such reasons for your opinions. Let those who ask your opinion be satisfied when they have got it. Yet, considering the great importance of the present inquiry, and the intense interest which it must excite, I will deviate from my ordinary practice.

Before stating this evidence, it must be observed, once for all, that though I hold that a sparkling wine similar to our best Champagne *was* known to the ancients, it is quite as clear that such was not a common characteristic of their wines. The resemblance was only of some of their choice vintages to those of our Champagnes. Otherwise, their wines were commonly still, strong, and often thick, like our "Essence Tokay." I do not care to trouble you with any learning on this head. It would be too large a dose for the present.

On all similar questions as to Grecian habits and Greek learning, the best and most universal authority is Athenæus. He is the most delightful and instructive author on matters of the table in any language, being to Greek literature a Dr. Kitchener of a higher order, or rather his work is what Brillat-Savarin's "Physiologie du Goût is in French;

but it is of far more value than Savarin's, because, with equal sprightliness and familiar knowledge of the subject that he handles, his book is filled, crammed, stuffed, spiced, larded with choice extracts from numerous Greek poets and dramatists, whose other writings are all lost.

I always make Athenæus my summer travelling companion—in the original, of course ; and I prefer reading him in Schweighauser's last edition, partly because it is the best, but chiefly because old Schweighauser was exceedingly kind to me at Strasbourg, more years ago than I care to tell. But as I know that your Greek is exceedingly rusty, *you* may consult Athenæus with profit and pleasure in Bohn's edition of Yonge's literal translation. I looked into it not long ago, and found that I could understand it nearly or quite as well as the original, which is more than I can say for most of the translations which our college lads use for "ponies."

Amongst an infinite number of delicious excerpts from Greek poets as popular in their day as Beranger is in our own, but of whom nothing remains to posterity but exquisite fragments, he quotes a long passage from Critias, who thus begins a poem which, by the way, is palpably the model of the well-known lines of Goethe, and of Byron who is thought to have borrowed from him. Yet as Byron knew much more Greek than he did German, I have no doubt that both he and Goethe copied directly from the old Greek. Byron has it thus :

"Know you the land of the cypress and myrtle ?"

Critias, addressing his native land of Sicily, says :

> " Hail to the land of the dim Proscrpine!
> There sparkles and foams the mirth-boding wine,
> With its froth, its fun and noise,
> Its folly, its wisdom, its joys—
> The folly of sages, the wisdom of boys."

Does not the " sparkling and foaming," etc., clearly refer to some everffescent, frothing wine ?

Again, Athenæus quotes various passages from Alexis, who seems to have been a Lesbian Tom Moore, for he luxuriates over " the rich and rosy wine " of the island of Lesbos, and thus addresses Bacchus on this wine:

> "Hail vine-crowned Bacchus, chief divine,
> Who from his sea-girt Lesbian lair
> Erst floated out the demon Care
> With sparkling, ruby wine."

Can there be any reasonable doubt that the " sparkling ruby wine," with its proper concomitant, " the floating out of old Care " from the place where he had long nestled in gloomy security, all allude to a choice, effervescing, red wine, precisely of the quality of an excellent *vin rosé mousseux de Champagne ?*

Then gushes forth a torrent of quotations out of the inexhaustible memory of this philosopher of good suppers, from the poet Hermippus, who seems a cosmopolitan sort of a bard, and writes as if he were at home over all the known world.   Complimenting other wines, for which he had unquestionably a right liberal and Catholic faith, the poet after praising the "Thasian's mild perfume," bursts into admiration of

>——" The bloom that mantles high
> O'er Homer's Chian cup."

In every one of these beautiful fragments you perceive the mantling, *pettilant* character of our best Champagne *mousseux* or *demi-mousseux*, and there are clear indications (in the original, at least) of the golden color of some of these sparkling vintages, and the roseate tinge of others.

By the way, there is another ancient usage of which Athenæus has preserved the memory together with that, dozens of authers where very names would have been swept into oblivion with their poems, their songs, ballads, their comedies which were once the charm of the civilized world had it not been for the inexhaustible memory of this most catholic of quoters. The fact may not be conclusive, but it is at least corroborative of the opinion I maintain.

It is that the Greeks were accustomed to cool their wines even by *snow*, as they were not blest with our ice houses. What is this but an anticipation of the *Vin de Champagne Frappe* of our modern tables.

I must content myself with only one more authority from this source. Athenæus himself, in his sober, prose speculations, says (Lib. 1, § 59) of a certain wine; "This kind is a wine which has a tendency to mount upward."

Now, with all deference to my old friend Schweighauser (who quite overlooks the point), how can any of the above passages be explained without understanding them to refer to wines resembling our sparkling Champagne?

If I thought that you could read Greek with any sort of facility, I should not have troubled you with the above imperfect but not unfaithful versions of these precious fragments. They are more faithful than those of Bohn's translation, if not more poetical; yet, like his, they are far from expressing the force and truth of the original. In reading aloud these exquisite fragments in their native Greek, I hear the whizzing burst of the exploded cork, I see the foaming froth of the goblet, I scent the flowery perfume of its delicate *bouquet*.

These and other authorities in Athenæus and the bright dramatists and poets whose gems the philosopher has preserved in his sober prose, like pearls in amber, are quite sufficient for my argument as to the Greek. When I get home among my books, I am sure that I can fortify these authorities by many passages to the same effect, from Plato, Aristotle, Ptolemæus, Hippocrates and St. Chrysostom.

Yet there is one other authority not to be omitted in such a discussion. It is even that of old Homer himself. In some thirty or more passages he paints his gods or heroes gazing upon the angry sea, to which he gives the epithet οἶνοψ, literally "wine-faced." The translators and commentators tell us that the compound word means "dark," or "ruddy," like the wine of that age. What stupidity! Is it not clear that it refers to the foam-covered deep—that it paints the angry main with its whole surface instinct with life, and mantling and foaming like the best foaming wine of the times—probably like that "Chian wine," that the poetic fragments in Athenæus tells us was Homer's favorite brand. In brief, the only translation which can convey the force of the epithet to a modern is the "Champagne-like deep" It is possible to describe more happily the "foam-faced sea," the οἶνοπα πόντον on which Achilles gazes, and calls forth his sea-born mother, in the beginning of the Epic story. How admirably does this harmonize with the wild spirit of the hero, and the stormy tale of his wrath and his glory. It becomes nearly as flat as the leavings of yesterday's uncorked Champagne, if this glowing epithet is reduced to "dark," or "ruddy," or even to "claret-colored,"—which last would be at least more poetical, though not more acurate.

Next, then, for the Romans. That a delicate *vin mousseux petillant*, a foaming and sparkling wine, was familiar to the tastes of the refined gentlemen of Rome in the time of Mæcenas and his little senate of poets, and soldiers, and philosophers, we need no better proof than the testimony of Virgil himself, who graphically represents the drinking of just such a wine as that with which you oblige your friends at various prices, and under sundry brands but all choice and dear. I take first the literal meaning of Virgil's melodious verses, though I have long thought that those contained a deeper secondary and recondite

sense, referring to the *recherché* repasts of Virgil's great
friend and patron, Mæcenas.   It is in the close of the first
book of the Æneid, in the recital of Dido's royal banquet
to the Trojan chief.   Toward the end of the feast, Dido
is described as ordering, and receiving, and filling with
wine, the hereditary massive goblet of gold and gems,
used by her progenitor Belus, and the long line of her
ancestors,

> " Hic Regina gravem gremmis auroque poposcit,
> Implevitque mero, pateram, quam Belus et omnes
> A Belo soliti "—

Then, after a pause of silence, she invokes Jove, the God
of hospitable laws, to make that day auspicious alike to
the wanderers of Troy and her own subjects exiles from
Tyre.   After inviting the favorable presence of Bacchus,
the giver of mirth, and of the gracious Juno, next she
pours on the table the liquid honors of libation (*laticum
libavit honorem*); and after touching the bowl with her
lip, passes it on with gay chiding at his slowness, to her
next neighbor Bitias.   Wherenpon,

> —— " Ille impiger hausit
> *Spu mantem* pateram, et pleno *se proluit* auro."

For the sake of being very accurate, I have given you
an exact prose version of the preceding lines, instead of
my own resounding translation; still, as I have already
informed you, in the press of Ticknor & Fields.   I
proceed in the same way as to those last quoted.   " He

(Bitias), no slouch at his glass—(none of the translators in any tongue, have given the sense of *impiger* with such precision), drained off the foaming cup, and bathed himself in the overflowing gold." Here, again, so far as I can remember, no one of the translators or commentators—I have examined all of them in my time, though not very lately—has given the full force of the "*pleno se proluit auro*," for though it implies that this inexpert drinker drenched himself with the choice liquor contained in the golden goblet, it also unquestionably means that he bathed his face in that vinous spray with which frothing Champagne often moistens or even bathes the face of the hasty and ill-mannered drinker. Good Abbé De Lille, better accustomed to the pleasures of Champagne than the port-drinking English translators and the beer-loving German commentators, comes much nearer in his

> " S'abreuvant à longs traits du nectar écumant."

But you will see how much better even than this I shall do it in my translation, which, as I have announced at least twice before, is now in press.

Here, then, I may triumphantly rest my argument. Yet I cannot refrain from adding what is probably known to very few scholars out of Italy. It is this; Cardinal Mai, whose services to learning have entitled him to the lasting gratitude of all scholars, discovered, eighteen months ago, among the hitherto unexplored treasures of the Vatican library, a manuscript, as yet unprinted, containing the Æneid with the notes of an anonymous old commentator or scholiast, evidently nearly contemporary with the poet, or at least of the very next generation to him, full of curious criticism and still more curious facts. This old scholiast, in his note on the very passage just under consideration, confirms a conjecture of my own, which I communicated in a paper of mine to the "London Classical Journal" some twelve years ago or more. He expressly says that this passage was meant to be understood in its literal sense by ordinary readers and by posterity, but that it also referred, in its interior or esoteric sense, to the habits of Mæcenas at his festive board, where Horace, Pollio, Varrus and Virgil were in the habit of dining with him twice every week, not including his birthday parties and other high festivities. On these occasions those favorite guests were always treated with a certain foaming wine of the "Dido brand"—"*vino effervescent, spumanteque, amphoris notâ Didonis signatis.*"

He adds, also, that this wine was always supplied for the table of Mæcenas from the wine-vaults of Sulpicius, "*Sulpicianis horreis,*" the same eminent wine-merchant whose stock is mentioned with great reverence by Horace in one of his odes.

As far as I can make out the topography of old Rome, Sulpicius had his chief commercial establishment in Curtius street, nearly opposite to the first city station of the great Appian Way, the Hudson River Railroad of

11

old Rome, a locatity not very unlike yours in your own city.

I trust that you are now quite satisfied that the gentlemen of Greece and Rome were accustomed to quaff a generous and pure *vin mousseaux*, quite like, and in no way inferior to the best Champagne of our times. I trust, also, that you will have ambition and patriotism enough to make the resemblance between old imperial Rome and your commercial Rome still more perfect by arranging with your correspondents at Rheims or at Cincinnati to supply you with a DIDO brand of the very choicest quality. Recollect that it must *not* be *non mousseux* or still, or even merely *crémaut*, but resembling as near as may be the Dido wine of antiquity, *spumans, petillant, mousseux,* sparkling, foaming, fragrant, and with the more important qualities of a delicate aroma and *an unimpeachable boquet.*

Yours, very truly, ——— ———.

P.S.—Remember me to our friend Dr. Francis, and congratulate him for me, on the honor of the legal doctorate so worthily added last month to his medical dignity by his venerable and distinguished Alma Mater. She has anticipated our university in this grateful duty. Yet I trust that our governing powers will not neglect to add his name to the list of those eminent persons educated elsewhere, but crowned with our academic laurel, who figure in our tri-ennial catalogue.

By the way, why does not the doctor, in his capacity of the Herodotus of your local history, amongst the fossil remains of the last century which he has dishumed, make out to dig up some choice reminiscences (there must have been much material for such) of the long residence of Brileat-Savarin in New York between sixty and seventy years ago. I was exceedingly interested with the account of him related by Mr. ———— in my visit to the Century Club, with you the last time I was in your city. That the immortal author of the great work on Transcendental Gastronomy should have lived for some years in New York, by scraping the violin in the humble and unscientific orchestra of the John street and Park Theatres, under the rule of Dunlap or Price, and then emerged in Paris the most successful of authors, the gayest and of table philosophers, and, moreover, a Judge of the Court of Cassation, the highest tribunal of France, promoted to that high station by the discriminating Napoleon, and continued by the Bourbons, is as whimsical and as surprising a vicissitude of fortune as any of the incidents in the life of Louis Philippe or of Louis Napoleon. I must unquestionably have seen him more than once in former days, at the Court of Cassation, seated by the side of his venerable chief, the Legitimist *Premier President* De Seze, and there affirming or reversing the decisions of the courts below, involving millions of francs and the most thorny points of the Code. But I never could dream that amongst these dignified

sages of the law, in their grave customary robes and ju-
dicial caps *á mortier*, I saw the sprightly author of the
"Physiology of Taste," who had erst for two or more
years been first violin of the only theatre in village-like
New York during the play-going days of your grandfather.

XXII.

German Wines, and a Wine Cellar.[*]

U p the Rhine in the leafy month of June, one might go further and fare worse, especially with regard to wine. The fact is, it is a noble thing to find some good in one's surroundings. To pass serenely and quietly from Claret, Burgundy and Champagne to Schiedam Schnapps and thence to Johannesberger, Marcobrunner, Rüdesheimer, and even Piesporter, without a groan. To take a glass of Completer at Coire or allay thirst by Vin de Glacier, Yvorne, or St. Georges, through the land of snow-capped mountains and yodles ; thence descending to d'Asti, Barbera, Campidano di Lombardi, Canonao del Sardegna, Monte Fiascone, Orvietto and Lagrima Christi ; drinking Aguardiente, Sherry and Val de Peñas in Spain, coming down to Bouza in Cairo or Mahayah in Morocco, pitching into Vodke or Kisslyschtxhy in Russia. Behold, QUO DUCIT GULA !

Perhaps, for euphony, it is the best way to sum up German wines under the headings Rhine wine, Moselle wine or the popular hock ; for what Anglo-Saxon head

---

[*] See Preface.

can always recall even a few names like Augenscheimer,
Assmannhaüser, Affenthaler, Bacharach, Brauneberger,
Bischeimer, Bessingheimer, Bodenheimer, Bechebacher,
Berncasther, Deidesheimer, Epsteiner, Euchariusberger,
Geissenheimer, Graacher, Grüenhauser, Hochheimer,
Hinterhaus, Johannesberger, Liebfrauenmilch, Lauben-
heimer, Liestener, Mittelheimer, Marcobrunner, Nier-
steiner, Oppenheimer, Pitcher, Rüdesheimer, Rauen-
thaler, Schamet, Steinberger, Steinwein, Schiersteiner,
Thiergartner, Walporger and Zeltingener?

It is a popular fallacy to suppose good German wines
are acid; they are dry, fine flavored, and keep better
than the five hundred year immortality of an oil paint-
ing. As for the alcohol in them, by a careful analysis,
Hochheimer showed only 14.37 per cent. of pure alcohol,
while a very old sample, only marked 8.8, a lower figure
than almost any of the French wines.

Johannesberger from the Schloss, is the king of German wines; twenty-five years ago, Mumm and Giesler
of Cologne and Johannesberg, held the vintage of 1822
at the rate of $10 per gallon; at compound interest it
would now be worth about $60 per gallon! This wine
with Steinberger, Geissenheimer and Hochheimer, have
the most delicate flavor and aroma of all German wines.
The warmest seasons insure the best vintages, so those
of 1748, 1766, 1779, 1783, 1800, 1802 and 1811 were
celebrated among the past generation as we now look to
1834, 1839, 1842 and 1846. Pure air and plenty of sun-

light are the best guardians for vines, and those crowning the high lands yield wine of the best body, while those in the low lands are poorer, and the wine requires years to attain a really fine flavor. Next to Johannesberger comes Steinberger of the Duke of Nassau, the iron hand in a velvet glove, delicate as a zephyr, it has the strength of a hurricane; kiss the beauty, but don't arouse the virago. *Hercules viraginem vicit*, but every one is not a "Dutchman!"

There is something very attractive in Liebfrauenmilch; the best comes from Worms, it has a good body and should be drunk reflectively, this milk for babes. While Marcobrunner, Rudesheimer and Niersteiner are for arms and the sword song of Körner.

Brauneberger ranks first among Moselle wines, and according to young Germany, there is not a headache in a hogshead of it; certainly after two bottles of it, there was no *kazenjammer* next morning. The old story that Bacchus, when he lived in the Father-land, having invited Jupiter down stairs to make a night of it on Brauneberger, so pleased the latter with this tipple, that he at once ordered all he could buy, on credit, for Olympus, to take the place of nectar, for a change; may be true. When you go to Heidelburg, stop at the Black Eagle Hotel, and ask Herr Lehr, the landlord, for a bottle of Sparkling White Moselle; drink it in the court-yard under the vine leaves, and to the sound of that fountain where the large trouts swim!

To look forward for ten years to seeing a cellar and then have it turn out a "sell," is one of the agonies of travel. Possibly under other circumstances, Auerbach's cellar in Leipsic would have worn less the air of a shows shop, or less like Julius Cæsar in peg-tops and a stove-pipe hat than I found it, but not even a bottle of Hoch-heimer—those paintings on the wall representing Faust's appearance and disappearance, and the old admonition of 1525:

"VIVE, BIBE, OBREGARE, MEMOR," etc.

could bring up anything ideal—so I left. At Mayence I was more favored, and though the scene comes up through several glasses dimly, at least the attempt can be made to describe an old-fashioned cellar, where travelling English don't ask "for that table, ah, he bored the holes in, you know. Faust, I mean. Three wax stoppers, and all that sort of thing?" "Haven't got it, sir!" answers the *kellner*. "Then why the — don't you make one!" says despairing England.

On the steamer from Coblentz, I formed the acquaint-ance of an officer, a lieutenant, who was just off duty from Ehrenbreitstein, and was on his way to Frankfort. Arriving after sunset, we determined to stay that night at Mayence, and go on next morning by railroad to Frankfort. After dinner at the hotel, we strolled out to look around town, and finally, as we crossed a narrow street, he proposed a bottle of Brauneberger in a cellar on the opposite side of the way, a quiet old nest, he said, where only old-fashioned and well-to-do Mayenzers were to be found. Down we went, and passing through an anteroom, where a fine specimen of a broad-shouldered middle-aged German was talking with a spectacled old gentleman with the air of a Professor, in a land where Professors are something; we were passing on to the next cellar, when the broad-shouldered landlord, bowing with great respect, saluted my companion with a string of titles as long as a roll of sausages. Upon which the Herr Professor, for such he was, lifted his hat politely to us, and, salutations over, we entered the next cellar attended by the landlord.

"Altmayer," said the officer, turning to him, "a bottle of *that* Brauneberger." And duly and deliberately the portly *wirth* departed, soon returning with the Moselle Nectar and glasses. If Hasenclever has not visited that cellar, he has sketched its match in some quaint old German city, for there it was, an interior worth crossing three oceans to sit in and drink Moselle or Rhine wine. The low ceiling was spanned with groined arches, dusky with age, not dark, as the *olla* color of Murillo, but a light-brown coffee-color, with a dash of light, borrowed from the lamp that hung in the centre of the cellar, and whose light just penetrated to the great butts lining the walls. The round table at which we were seated was of oak, dark with age, and anything more beautiful in the way of the light that shone through our brimming glasses of Brauneberger, and was reflected on that dark

oak, I have never seen. The *wirth* having returned to
the ante-room, my companion, evidently pleased with the
interest I took in the surroundings of the cellar, judi-
ciously kept silence until I had thoroughly viewed it all,
sipping slowly the delicate wine, and wondering how all
the sunlight got into the cellar at night. There was
positively a thin golden cloud all around us, and such
serene repose as a traveller who has been through a
dozen galleries of paintings, innumerable churches, etc.,
all in one day, believes to be the height of pleasure, *i. e.*,
KHEYF!

" I am very glad we came here," said the lieutenant,
"for I see you can appreciate what I have always
thought one of the most picturesque wine cellars in this
part of Germany. Have you noticed the grotesque
carving on that door leading to the further cellar?"
Turning my head in the direction indicated, I noticed a
pointed arch doorway, surrounded with the most beautiful
gothic tracery leaves, birds, monkeys, grapes, curious
grinning heads, all cut in stone, while the oak panels of
the door were rich in carved flowers and leaves.

" The oak door," said the lieutenant, "is a modern
addition of the *wirth's*, but the rest runs back to the
16th century." While I was still looking at the curious
carving round the door, three or four middle-aged gentlemen, together with the spectacled Professor, entered
the cellar, and after polite salutations, drew up to the
table, and the *wirth* soon appeared with bottles and

glasses for the different private guests, for in such light they all appeared and acted. Having a cigar case well stocked with a supply of Partagas *primeras*, it went the rounds, and the cigars were accepted after much urging on my part, for the idea is not German; I had the satisfaction of reaping an amount of gratified expressions from each smoker that paid me for the sacrifice; for I had nursed the few I brought with me from the States with great care. Conversation flowed on easily, and the second bottle of Brauneberger went the way of the first; it was even better nectar than its leader. The light in the cellar appeared brighter and brighter, the golden cloud seemed filled with bees-wings humming, the great butts looming out of the mellow light looked like brown Franciscans making merry over a bottle of *sambuca*. The spectacled Professor told a right good story two feet broad, the other elderly gentlemen kept it up! The lieutenant ordered a third bottle of Brauneberger, which was better than its predecessors.

Then there came in a wandering violin-player, blind as a bat, and a very pretty girl with a guitar, who was not blind, as her bright eyes, shining on the handsome lieutenant, plainly told, and when she sung that pretty song of "Frau Nachtigal," it appeared to me, after the wine, that she accented those lines—

> " Wer du bist, der bin auch ich,
> | : Drum lass nach—zu lieben mich " : |

and regarded the lieutenant in the adoring style, permitting, at some future time, any amount of *poussir*ing, as the Germans have it. Then we ordered just one more bottle of Brauneberger, and the lieutenant, taking the guitar from the pretty girl, sung in a fine, baritone voice, "Soldatenleben"—

"Kein besser Leben,
Ist ouf dieser Welt zu denken "—

and the old gentlemen joined in the "Valleri, vallera, valle-ra!" chorus with hearty good will and *kreutz fidélely!*

Several glasses of wine were bestowed on the blind violinist, a collection made for the pretty girl, who assured the lieutenant her name was Aennchen von Tharau, which he doubted, insisting on it that Aennchen died in 1659, and lived in Himmel Strasse! But she gave us a parting song, prettily sung, and floated off into that golden cloud and hum of bees, and the old Franciscans smiled away from the big butts, and the spectacled Professor bore us backward in his discourse to the days when men passed whole lives as we were now passing hours, and believed they were doing right, the illiterate heathen.

"The Herr Professor will have us in Egyptian bondage directly, unless we hurry away," said the lieutenant to me in a low voice; so we arose, as arise men who bear away many bottles; and kindly greetings and adieux bore us off to the *wirth*, who hoped to see us soon again, and bestowed all the titles on my companion that he had inherited and won ; and we sailed out into the moonlit streets of Mayence, and down to the hotel by the arrowy Rhine, and slept the sleep of men who have drank good Brauneberger in a grand old cellar surrounded by refined and genial companions.

VALE !

XXIII

A Christmas Piece

of garnered rhyme, from hidden stores of olden time, that since the language did begin, have welcomed merry Christmas in, and made the winter nights so long, fleet by on wings of wine and song ; for when the snow is on the roof, the house within is sorrow proof, if yule clog blazes on the hearth, and cups and hearts o'er-brim with mirth. Then bring the wassail to the board, with nuts and fruit—the winter's hoard ; and bid the children take off shoe, to hang their stockings by the flue ; and let the clear and frosty sky, set out its brightest jewelry, to show old Santa Claus the road, so he may ease his gimcrack load. And with the coming of these times, we'll add some old and lusty rhymes, that suit the festive season well, and sound as sweet as Christmas bell. And here's a stave from rare old Ben, who wrote with most melodious pen :

> To the old, long life and treasure ;
> To the young, all health and pleasure :
> To the fair, their face
> With eternal grace ;
> And the soul to be loved at leisure.

To the witty, all clear mirrors;
To the foolish, their dark errors;
    To the loving sprite,
    A secure delight;
To the jealous, their own false terrors.

And here's from that Bricklayer's pate, a stave that's most appropriate; for when the Christmas chimes begin, to eat and drink we count no sin; as sexton at the rope doth pull, it cries, "Oh, bell! bell! bell-y-full!"

HYMN.

Room! room! make room for the Bouncing Belly,
First father of sauce, and deviser of jelly;
Prime master of art, and the giver of wit,
That found out the excellent engine the spit;
The plough and the flail, the mill and the hopper,
The hutch and the boulter, the furnace and copper,
The oven, the boven, the mawken, the peel,
The hearth and the range, the dog and the wheel;
He, he first invented the hogshead and tun,
The gimlet and vice, too, and taught them to run,
And since with the funnel and hippocras bag,
He has made of himself, that he now cries swag!

Now just bethink of castle gate, where humble midnight mummers wait, to try if voices, one and all, can rouse the tipsy seneschal, to give them bread and beer and brawn, for tidings of the Christmas morn; or bid each yelper clear his throat, with water of the castle moat; for thus they used, by snow and torch, to rear their voices at the porch:

Wassail! wassail! all over the town,
Our toast it is white, and our ale it is brown;
Our bowl is made of a maplin tree;
We be good fellows all;—I drink to thee.

Here's to our horse,* and to his right ear,
God send our measter a happy new year;
A happy new year as e'er he did see,—
With my wassailing bowl I drink to thee.

Here's to our mare, and to her right eye,
God send our mistress a good Christmas pie;
A good Christmas pie as e'er I did see,—
With my wassailing bowl I drink to thee.

Here's to our cow, and to her long tail,
God send our measter us never may fail
Of a cup of good beer: I pray you draw near,
And our jolly wassail it's then you shall hear.

Be here any maids? I suppose here be some;
Sure they will not let young men stand on the cold stone!
Sing hey O. maids! come trole back the pin,
And the fairest maid in the house let us all in.

Come, butler, come, bring us a bowl of the best;
I hope your soul in heaven will rest;
But if you do bring us a bowl of the small,
Then down fall butler, and bowl and all.

And here's a Christmas carol meant for children, and most excellent, and though the monk that wrote it was hung, yet still his verses may be sung.

---

* In this place, and in the first line of the following verse, the name of the horse is generally inserted by the singer; and "Filpail" is often substituted for "the cow" in a subsequent verse.

A CAROL BY ROBERT SOUTHWELL.

As I in a hoarie, winter's night
  Stood shivering in the snow,
Surpriz'd I was with sudden heat,
  Which made my heart to glow;
And lifting up a fearefull eye
  To view what fire was neere,
A prettie babe, all burning bright,
  Did in the aire appeare;
Who, scorchèd with excessive heat,
  Such flouds of teares did shed,
As though his flouds should quench his flames,
  Which with his teares were bred:
Alas! (quoth he) but newly borne,
  In fierie heats I frie,
Yet none approach to warm their hearts,
  Or feele my fire, but I;
My faultlesse brest the furnace is,
  The fuell, wounding thornes:
Love is the fire, and sighs the smoke,
  The ashes, shames and scornes;
The fuell justice layeth on,
  And mercy blows the coales,
The metalls in this furnace wrought,
  Are Men's defiled soules:
For which, as now on fire I am,
  To work them to their good,
So will I melt into a bath,
  To wash them in my blood.
With this he vanisht out of sight,
  And swiftly shrunke away,
And straight I called unto minde
  That it was Christmasse Day.

And here's a song so pure and bright, it may be read
on Christmas night, unless the moon her light do lack,
for which consult the almanac:

12

A HYMN TO DIANA.

Queen and huntress, chaste and fair,
  Now the sun is laid to sleep,
Seated in thy silver chair,
  State in wonted manner keep ;
    Hesperus entreats thy light,
    Goddess, excellently bright.

Earth, let not thy envious shade,
  Dare itself to interpose,
Cynthia's shining orb was made ·
  Heaven to clear, when day did close :
    Bless us, then, with wished right,
    Goddess, excellently bright.

Lay thy bow of pearl apart,
  And thy crystal-shining quiver ;
Give unto the flying hart,
  Space to breathe, how short soever ;
    Thou, that makest a day of night,
    Goddess, excellently bright.

And here is something quaint and tough, for such as have not had enough : a Christmas carol, that was done in 16 hundred twenty 1 :

ANE SANG OF THE BIRTH OF CHRIST.

With the tune of *Baw lula law.*
(*Angelus, ut opinor, loquitur.*)

I come from Hevin to tell,
The best Nowellis that ever befell :
To yow thir Tythinges trew I bring,
And I will of them *say* and sing.

  This Day to yow is borne ane Childe,
Of Marie meik ane Virgine mylde,
That *blisset Barne* bining and kynde
Sall yow rejoyce baith Heart and Mynd.

My Saull and Lyfe stand up and see
Quha *lyes* in ane *Cribe* and *Tree*,
Quhat Babe is that so gude and faire?
It is Christ, God's Sonne and *Aire*.

O God that made all Creature,
How art thow becum so pure,
That on the Hay and Stray will lye,
Amang the *Asses*, *Oxin*, and *Kye?*

O my deir Hert, zoung Jesus sweit,
Prepare thy *Creddil* in my *Spreit*,
And I sall *rocke thee* in my *Hert*,
And never mair from thee depart.

But I sall praise thee ever moir
With Sangs sweit unto thy Gloir,
The *Knees* of my *Hert* sall I *bow*,
And sing that richt *Balulalow*.*

And here are several hints to show, how Christmas
customs first did grow, for as the holy fathers say, some
Pagan tricks we Christians play, and prove that Yule and
Christmas box, are not precisely orthodox, for so we quote
and understand,

ANTIQUITIES FROM FATHER BRAND.

In the *Primitive Church*, Christmas-Day was always
observed as the *Lord's-Day* was, and was in like Man-

---

* The Rev. Mr. Lamb, in his entertaining notes on the old poem on
the Battle of Flodden Field, tells us that the nurse's lullaby song,
balow, (or "he balelow,") is literally French. "*Hè bas! la le loup!*"
that is, "hush! there's the wolf!"

ner preceded by an *Eve or Vigil.* Hence it is that our Church hath ordered an *Eve* before it, which is observed by the Religious, as a Day of Preparation for that great Festival.

Our Fore-Fathers, when the common Devotions of the *Eve* were over, and Night was come on, were wont to light up *Candles* of an uncommon Size, which were called *Christmas-Candles,* and to lay a *Log* of Wood upon the fire, which they termed a *Yule-Clog* or *Christmas-Block.* These were to Illuminate the House, and turn the Night into Day; which Custom, in some Measure, is still kept up in the Northern Parts.

The Apostles were *the Light of the World;* and as our Saviour was frequently called *Light,* so was his Coming into the World signified, and pointed out by the Emblems of Light: "It was then," (says our Countryman *Gregory*) "the longest Night in all the Year; and it was the midst of that, and yet there was Day where he was: For a glorious and betokening Light shined round about this *Holy Child.* So says Tradition, and so the Masters describe the Night Piece of the Nativity." If this be called in Question, as being only Tradition, it is out of Dispute, that the Light which illuminated the Fields of *Bethlehem,* and shone round about the *Shepherds* as they were watching their Flocks, was an Emblem of that Light, which was then come into the World. "What can be the Meaning," says *venerable Bede,* "that this Apparition of Angels was surrounded with that heavenly Light,

which is a Thing we never meet with in all the Old
Testament? For tho' Angels have appeared to Prophets
and holy Men, yet we never read of their Appearing in
such Glory and Splendor before. It must surely be, because this Privilege was reserved for the Dignity of this
Time. For when the true Light of the World, was born
in the World, it was very proper that the Proclaimer of
His Nativity, should appear in the Eyes of Men, in such
an heavenly Light, as was before unseen in the World.
And that *supernatural Star*, which was the Guide of the
Eastern Magi, was a Figure of that *Star*, which was
risen out of *Jacob ; of that Light which should lighten the*
Gentiles." " God," says Bishop *Taylor*, " sent a miracu-
lous Star, to invite and lead them to a new and more
glorious Light, the Light of Grace and Glory."

In Imitation of this, as *Gregory* tells us, the Church
went on with the Ceremony : And hence it was, that for
the three or four First *Centuries*, the whole *Eastern
Church* called the Day, which they observed for our
Saviour's Nativity, the *Epiphany* or Manifestation of the
Light. And *Cassian* tells us, that it was a Custom in
Egypt, handed down by Tradition, as soon as the *Epiphany*, or *Day of Light* was over, &c. Hence also came
that ancient Custom of the same Church, taken Notice of
by St. *Jerome*, of lighting up Candles at the Reading of
the Gospel, even at Noon-Day ; and that, not to drive
away the Darkness, but to speak their Joy for the good
Tidings of the Gospel, and be an Emblem of that Light,

which the Psalmist says, *was a Lamp unto his Feet and a Light unto his Paths.*

The *Yule-Dough* (or *Dow*), was a kind of *Baby* or *little Image of Paste*, which our Bakers used formerly to bake at this Season, and *present* to their *Customers*, in the same manner as the Chandlers gave *Christmas Candles.* They are called *Yule-Cakes* in the county of Durham. I find in the antient Calendar of the Romish Church, that at Rome, on the Vigil of the Nativity, *Sweetmeats* were *presented* to the *Fathers* in the *Vatican*, and that all Kinds of *little Images* (no doubt of *Paste*) were to be found at the Confectioners' Shops.

There is the greatest Probability that we have had from *hence* both our *Yule-Doughs* and *Mince Pies*, the latter of which are still in common Use at this Season. The *Yule-Dough* has perhaps been intended for an *Image* of the *Child Jesus.* It is now, if I mistake not, pretty generally laid aside, or at most retained only by Children.

J. Boëmus Aubanus tells us, that in Franconia, on the three Thursday Nights preceding the *Nativity* of our Lord, it is customary for the Youth of both Sexes to go from *House* to *House*, *knocking* at the *Doors*, *singing* their *Christmas Carrols*, and *wishing a happy new Year.* They get in Return from the Houses they stop at, *Pears*, *Apples*, *Nuts*, and even *Money.*

Little Troops of Boys and Girls still go about in this very Manner at Newcastle, some few Nights before, on the Night of the *Eve* of this Day, and on that of the *Day itself.* The *Hagmena** is still preserved among them. They still *conclude*, too, with wishing "a *merry Christ, mas*, and a *happy new Year.*"

We are told in the Athenian Oracle, that the *Christmas Box Money* is derived from hence. The Romish Priests had Masses said for almost every Thing: If a ship went out to the Indies, the Priests had a *Box* in her under the Protection of some Saint: And for Masses, as their Cant was, to be said for them to that Saint, &c., the poor People must put in something into the Priests' Box, which is not to be opened till the Ship return.

The *Mass* at that time was called *Christmas ;* the *Box, Christmas Box*, or *Money* gathered against that Time, that *Masses* might be made by the Priests to the Saints to *forgive* the *people* the *Debaucheries* of *that Time ;* and from this Servants had the *Liberty to get Box Money*, that *they too* might be *enabled* to *pay* the *Priest* for his *Masses*, knowing well the Truth of the Proverb :

"No Penny, No Pater-noster."

Another Custom observed at this Season, is the adorning of Windows with *Bay* and *Laurel.* It is but seldom observed in the North, but in the Southern-Parts it is very Common, particularly at our *Universities ;* where it is Customary to adorn, not only the Common Windows

---

* Hagmena—*i.e.*, Haginmeene, holy month.

of the *Town*, and of the *Colleges*, but also to bedeck the *Chapels* of the *Colleges*, with *Branches of Laurel*.

The *Laurel* was used among the ancient *Romans*, as an Emblem of several Things, and in particular, of *Peace*, and Joy, and Victory. And I imagine, it has been used at this Season by Christians, as an Emblem of the same Things; as an Emblem of Joy for the Victory gain'd over the Powers of Darkness, and of that *Peace on Earth*, *that Good-will towards Men*, which the Angels sung over the Fields of *Bethlehem*.

It has been made use of by the *Non Conformists*, as an Argument against Ceremonies, that the second Council of *Bracara*, *Can.* 73, forbad Christians " *to deck their Houses with Bay Leaves and Green Boughs*." But the Council does not mean, that it was wrong in Christians to make use of these Things, but only "at *the same Time with the Pagans*, *when they observed and solemnized their Paganish Pastime and Worship*. And of this Prohibition, they give this Reason in the same *Canon*; *Omnis hæc observatio paganismi est*. All this kind of Custom doth hold of Paganism: Because the outward Practice of *Heathenish Rites*, perform'd jointly with the Pagans themselves, could not but imply a Consent in Paganism."

But at present, there is no hazard of any such Thing. It may be an Emblem of Joy to us, without confirming any, in the practice of *Heathenism*. The *Time*, the *Place*, and the *Reasons* of the *Ceremony*, are so widely different, that, tho' formerly, to have observed it, would unquestionably have been a Sin, it is now become harmless, comely, and decent.

So here we close our prose and rhyme, and end the Chrismas pantomime, with wishing health and happy cheer, to you through all the coming year, and prosperous times in every State, for eighteen hundred sixty-eight.

XXIV.

Oxyporian Wines.*

W E have received from our esteemed friend, and
valued correspondent, whose paper on the
champagne wines of the ancients excited so much surprise and curiosity in literary circles, another article
upon kindred topics, which will no doubt prove even
more interesting than the former one. Embracing, as
it does, a wider range of inquiry, it exhibits more clearly
than the other paper, unusual stores of scholarship, at
once comprehensive, familiar, and accurate; a vigorous
and telling style—in itself a model of good English
writing; a curious and technical knowledge of wines in
general, beyond that of any modern writer with whom
we are familiar, an exact knowledge of chemistry, and a
happy vein of humor, as original as it is genuine. It is
not surprising that the authorship of the last paper
should have been ascribed to several of the most profound
scholars in the country. But we can safely predicate of
this one that it will excite a still wider range of speculation as to the name of the writer, which, for the present,

* See Preface.

we shall withhold until such time as we are permitted to print it.

THE LETTER.

———, October 5, 1860.

MY DEAR EDITOR:—I have been much amused in learning through the press, as well as from the more sprightly narrative of your private letter, that such and so very odd claims and conjectures had been made as to the authorship of my late hasty letter to you, in proof that the poets and gentlemen of old Greece and Rome drank as good champagne as we do. You know very well that the letter which you published was not originally meant for the public, and the public have no right at all to inquire who the author may be; nor, indeed, has the said impertinent public to inquire into the authorship of any anonymous article which harms nobody, nor means to do so. I have not sought concealment in this matter, nor do I wish notoriety. If any one desires the credit of the communication, such as it is, he or she is quite welcome to it until I find leisure to prepare for the press a collection of my Literary Miscellanies under my own name. I intend to embody in it an enlarged edition of this essay on the antiquity of *champagne mousseux*, with a regular chain of Greek and Latin authorities defending and proving all my positions.

To this future collection of my critical and philological writings I look forward with a just pride as a fit gift

to the few in our country who occupy their leisure, not
with light and trifling literature, but on grave and solid
studies (like the investigation of the Champagne question), and with the culture of high and recondite learning;
or, as this thought is admirably expressed by Petrarch,
in one of his epistles, announcing to a learned friend the
completion of one of his Latin prose works, in a passage which I have selected for the motto of my own
Collectanea: " Munus hocce prebeo, non iis qui levibus
et ludicris nugis assueti sunt, sed lis quibus cordi est,
gravis et severus bonarum literarum et doctrinæ recon-
ditæ cultus."

You tell me that you have every day personal inquiries
or written communications to the Wine Press, desiring
information as to the meaning of the word *Oxyporian*,
which I used as characterizing the effects of certain
wines. It seems that the word is in neither of the rival
American dictionaries, nor in any English one in present
use. Of this I was not aware, but if it is not in their
dictionaries, so much the worse for the learned lexicographers. It ought to have been there; they have
no excuse for omitting it. On the other hand, you and
I deserve all such honor as the literary and scientific
public can bestow, for restoring the word Oxyporian to
the present generation. It is a good word, and one—as
Corporal Bardolph phrases it—" of exceeding good command." But I shall not imitate the gallant corporal in
his style of definition and explanation: "Accommodated!

that is, when a man is, as they say, accommodated; or
when a man is—being—whereby—he may be thought to
be accommodated, which is an excellent thing." That is
not *my* fashion. This word OXYPORIAN is of great
antiquity and high descent. It was first used by Hippocrates, and from his medical use passed to that of the
philosophers, thence into the Latin, and thence to the
old English medical and philosophical writers down to
Sydenham, since whose day it has not been used for near
two centuries. It is from the Greek Ὀξυπορίως and means
simply that which is of speedy operation and as quick in
passing off—first used as a substantive name of such a
medicine, then as an adjective with a broader sense. I am
sorry that it has gone out of fashion, for no other word
can supply its place, either for scientific or literary use.
The philosophy of the word, especially as applied to
wines, is nowhere better illustrated than by one of the
old lost poets in a fragment preserved by my favorite
Athenæus. The Athenian dramatist, Philyllius thus
describes the Oxyporian character and effects of certain
wines:

> Take Thasian, Chian, Mendian wine,
> Lesbian old or new Biblyne,
> Differing all, but all divine—
>
> Straight to the brain all swift ascend,
> Drive out black thoughts, bright fancies lend,
> Glad the whole man—then pass away
> Nor make to-morrow mourn *its* yesterday.

That last line cost me more labor than I have often
bestowed upon a whole lecture, and though it is hyper-
catelectic with redundant syllables, expressive enough, I
think of the metre and feeling of the original, it has not
done full justice to the crowded thought, the practical
philosophy of the gay and wise old heathen.

I never read Athenæus without renewed gratitude to
kind Professor Schweighauser, who first opened to me
that treasure-house of the remains of ancient bards,
"with whom (justly says a modern critic) perished so
much beauty as the world will never see again." How
fortunate it was that the old Greek philosophical diner-
out was as much given to quotation as Montaigne, Jere-
my Taylor or myself. As for the learned French-German
or German-Frenchman, Schweighauser—the recollections of my brief acquaintance with him rise in my mind
like "a steam of rich distilled perfumes," fraught with
the memory of refined classical criticism, and the flavor
of the world-renowned culinary product of his own
beloved city of Strasbourg, the *pâté de foies gras.*

But I must not forget to call your attention to the
very curious parallel between this fragment of an Athenian dramatic author and Falstaff's eulogy on the virtues
of his favorite sherris-sack. " It hath a twofold operation
in it. It ascends me into the brain, drives me forth all
the foolish, dull and crudy vapors which overrun it,
makes it apprehensive, quick, forgetive, full of nimble,
fiery and delectable shapes." "The second property of

your excellent sherris is the warming of the blood, which
before cold and settled left the liver white and cold, but
the sherris-sack warms it "—— Yet why need I quote
any more of what you and half your readers have by
heart. Now there is not the slightest ground for attrib-
uting this resemblance of thought and expression to
imitation. No, (as I remarked in one of my lectures on
the resemblances to be traced between Shakspeare and
the Greek tragedies), the great ancients and this greater
modern coincide in thought because they alike draw their
thoughts from truth and nature and the depths of man's
heart. The comparison of the passage cited from Falstaff and that of which I have above given my feeble
version, affords ample evidence of this. They agree
marvellously in describing the *immediate* operation of
the lighter Greek wines, resembling our best Bordeaux
and champagne, and that of Falstaff's more powerful
and grave sherry. In this they are equally true. But the
Greek goes on to insist on the Oxyporian worth of his
favorite wines in gladdening the whole man "with mirth
which after no repentance draws." Not so the great
English poet. He, with a dietetic and physiological
philosophy as profound and as accurate as was his insight
into the affections and passions of man, passes over in
profound silence this point on which the Greek bard
dwells. This Shakspeare does, not from ignorance, but
to lead the reader to infer from Falstaff's own infirmities,
that such was *not* the after-operation of Falstaff's "inor-

dinate deal of sack"—that his drink was not Oxyporian
—that did not pass away "like the baseless fabric of
a vision" (and, to use the words of the great bard in a
sense which he might not immediately have intended, but
which was, nevertheless, present to his vast intellect:)

—"Leave not a *rack* behind."

The fat knight experienced to the end of his days the
slow but sure operation of his profuse and potent beve-
rages, in results from which the judicious drinker of the
more delicate wines of modern France as well as of
ancient Ionia is and was wholly exempt.

But a truce to ideas of past ages. Let me come down
to our own day, and give you a practical example of the
use and value of this word Oxyporian, and the immense
benefit which we have conferred upon our own country-
men, in having thus followed the precept of Horace* and

* Proferet in fucem, spuiosa vocabula rerum,
Qune priscis memorata Catonibis ut que Cethegis,
Nunc situs informis premit et deserta re Juitus.

Horat. Epist. L. ii, r. 116.

so happily paraphrased and adapted to modern speech
by Pope:

"Command old words that long have slept to wake,
Words that wise Bacon or brave Raleigh spake."

Such a word was this same *Oxyporian*. Now mark
its application.

Suppose that by way of aiding and embellishing my Thanksgiving family festivities, you present me with a basket or two of sparkling native wine prepared according to the recently improved method. Thereupon I send you a brief certificate thus worded:

"I certify that I have tried (number of bottles left blank) of improved sparkling Catawba on self, family and friends, and find the same truly Oxyporian."

These few words speak volumes—a whole encyclopedia in that one word *Oxyporian*. Even with my humble name thereto subscribed, what an effect would this produce! But if in addition you could prevail on our mutual friend, Dr. Holmes, to concur with a similar attestation, how that effect would be multiplied a hundred fold! The professor, upon the exhibition of a proper quantum of the last edition of our best brands, would, doubtless, in the Macbeth spirit of his late anniversary discourse against chemicals and Galenicals, certify to this effect:

"After repeated experiments of the wine to me exhibited by F. S. C., being native sparkling Catawba, with last improvements, I certify the same to be eminently *Oxyporian*. Take this *quant. suffi.* Repeat the draught next day. 'Throw physic to the dogs."

"O. W. H."

I shall be much mistaken if such certificates, thus clear, strong, brief, inspiring public confidence and public thirst, would not at once compel our native cultivators to put hundreds of thousands of acres more into grape cul-

13

tivation, and oblige the sole agent in New York to hurry A. T. Stewart higher up Broadway, leaving that marble palace to be converted into an Oxyporian Hall for the exclusive sale of Catawba and other Oxyporian liquids, domestic and foreign.

The same experiments might with great propriety, and, doubtless, with equal success, be repeated upon Dr. Holmes and myself with the Dido brand of French champagne when it arrives.

I have just said that I am determined not to enter at present into verbal controversy on the accuracy of my translations and citations on the great question of the champagne of antiquity. I leave all that till my proposed publication, which I trust will settle the question, even against the authority of Eustathius and Gladstone as to the word οἴνωπα, though the one was a Greek archbishop eight hundred years ago, and the other is the present Chancellor of the Exchequer of the British Empire, and has just achieved the triumph of abolishing the duties on champagne and other wines of France.

But I learn that two other arguments have been advanced against my doctrine, both from distinguished quarters, and both founded, not upon the authority of scholiasts and lexicons, but upon the principles and reasoning of the higher criticism.

The first of these is advanced by President King, o f your New York Columbia College. His objection to my argument is briefly this : If either the Greeks or the

Romans had champagne, Horace must have taken his share, and luxuriated in recounting its merits and glories. As Horace makes not even a distant allusion to any wine of this kind, no such can have been in use in his days. I have a great respect for President King's judgment, both in respect to champagne and to Horace; and his argument is logical in form and plausible in reasoning. Still this must have been an *obiter dictum* of his (as the lawyers say), not a formal decision, such as he would have given on full argument and examination of the authorities. I think that I can convince the President of the error of his argument; and considering the magnitude of the question, and the responsibilities of his position, I am confident that he has too much candor to persist in his error after duly weighing my reasoning.

I object entirely to Horace's testimony—to his competence—if he is offered as an *expert* in wine; but if he is regarded as an ordinary witness to facts, then to the credibility, weight, or value of his negative testimony. This objection arises from no general disrespect to his character or talent. I am far from agreeing with an accomplished professor of your city, whom I might address in the words of Horace,

" Docte sermones utriusque linguæ,"

as master alike of the tongue of Shakspeare and of that of Schiller. I cannot agree with him in vilipending

Horace—to use a word of Charles Fox's, which I fancy has not been used since his days. I was told lately, at a literary party in Boston, by an eminent fellow-citizen of yours, that this accomplished New York professor had pronounced Horace to be "a mediocre old fogy." So do not I.

As a keen-sighted observer and describer of men and manners, full of shrewd good sense and worldly wisdom, Horace has no rival; and the unanswerable proof of it is that his thoughts and maxims, and even language, on such topics, have been incorporated into the thoughts, language, and best literature of all modern nations. In pure poetry, his patriotic pride and ardent love of country often raise him to the noblest strains of lyric declamation. Above all, he has an unrivalled power of natural but condensed expression, compressing whole pages of thought, or of description of nature, of form or of manner, into a short phrase or a brilliant word or two. On some other points I nearly agree with your professor, who is as polyglot in knowledge as he is in languages. Horace's love-verses I hold very cheap. In these he is indeed graceful, courtly, airy, elegant: but he has little passion and no tenderness. If he ever approaches to any semblance of either passion or affection, it is when he translates or imitates the Greek, to which source late German critics have traced not a few of his minor lyric beauties, and made it probable that he owed more than can now be clearly ascertained. The other line, in which I hold

him to be still more clumsy and out of his element, is that
which specially relates to our present purpose. It is that
which he often affects, and affects with little success, the
gaiety of the Bacchanalian songster. In nearly every
one of his convivial odes he is as far as possible from the
light gaiety or the broad jollity of such poets as Burns
or Béranger, and a dozen Scotch and Irish songsters of
far less name but of scarcely less merit. In his desperate
attempts at jollity, his constant incentive to festivity—
which seems to mean, with him, nothing but hard drinking—is the shortness of human life and the black prospect
of death, so that his festive odes may be condensed into
the thought of Captain Macheath, in the Beggar's Opera:

" A man will die bolder with brandy."

Much as in his "Moriture Delli," etc., he is inferior
to the gay songsters of later times, he appears still worse
when any of his scenes of conviviality are compared
with those of Shakspeare, of Cervantes, or of Scott,
with the feasts of Falstaff, of Sancho, or of Friar Tuck.
If I compare Horace with these moderns, it is because
the contrast is more striking from our familiarity with
the latter. But the same thing might be shown to
scholars by placing him by the side of Plutus, or of the
remains of Greek comedy. The truth is, that Horace,
with all his love of company, his shrewd observation of
life, his keen perception of the ridiculous, was decidedly
a melancholy man. I do not believe that in his most

convivial hours, he ever rung out that hearty peal of
laughter for which Walter Scott was celebrated; nor was
Horace, in those solitay rambles of his about the shops,
markets and by-places of Rome, which he so agreeably
relates, ever seen smiling and chuckling to himself, over
his own thick-coming pleasant fancies, like your Halleck,
when amusing himself in the same fashion in his frequent
visits to Boston or New York.

Yes, Horace was clearly as melancholy a man, when
by himself, as Lord Byron was, and for the same reason,
a stomach performing its functions badly, and stimulated
in the one case by Falernian, in the other by strong gin
and water.

Horace himself, unconsiously, shows us the philosophy
of all this, in the account which he gives here and there
of his own history. He had led a pretty hard, promis-
cuous sort of a life in his early days of inglorious and
disastrous military rank. Afterward he got up in the
world, and became the holder of a comfortable office, of
more profit than honor; and then, by the favor of his
friends in power, became a well-to-do country gentleman.
Next we find him suffering the certain penalties of an
early debauched and chronically debilitated stomach.
He had weak eyes, and a deranged digestion, the first
being the natural result of the other malady. He at
times resorted to total abstinence and cold water, and
became a great critic in good water, in which last particular he showed his usual practical good sense. He was

constantly running about, as he tells us, from the plain
fare of his Sabine farm to Rome, where he shared the
luxurious table of Mecænas. Thence he galloped off to
Baiæ, the Newport of that day; then from one mineral
spring to another; now dosing himself with chalybeate,
now with sulphur water. But all this water regimen is
interspersed with frolic after frolic in old Falernian. His
love of Falernian flashes the whole truth upon us. What
was this famed Falernian wine? It was, unquestionably,
a rich, high-flavored wine, but as unquestionably most
highly brandied, decidedly fortified with an enormous
proportion of alcohol, nearly bringing it up to the proof
of our most approved old cognac. The commentators
and compilers of antiquities do not let us into the secret
of this same famed Falernian. But I speak on the very
best authority. It is that of Pliny the naturalist.

In speaking of the strong Roman wines, he says of the
Falernian varieties, in a customary phrase of his, that
there is no wine of higher authority, "Nec ulli in vino
major auctoritas." He then adds, that it was inflamma-
ble! and the only wine that was so: "Solo vinorum
flamma accenditur." "It is the only kind from which
flame can be kindled." The ancients had no more precise test than this one, that of burning with a flame, to
ascertain the proportion of alcohol in these liquors. They
had nothing similar to the various beautiful modes of
modern chemistry, to ascertain the alcoholic proportions
of wine as the eboulliscope of the French chemists, the

halymetric method used by Fuchs and Zieri, and the
ingenious aerometer of Tabaric, all which give such
elegant precision to the alcoholic tables, digested and
enlarged by our exact Dutch friend, Professor Mulder.
But Pliny's statement is enough to prove that the strength
of Falernian did not arise from "combined alcohol"
formed in the natural process of fermentation of the
grape juice, but from added "uncombined alcohol" (as
the chemists term it) produced by distillation. On this
very question, I cannot refrain from quoting the opinion
of Dr. Watson, of New York, in his most agreeable,
learned and instructive work on "The Medical Profession
in Ancient Times," a volume which, if it had been published in London, would have been reprinted in the
United States, and had a circulation of thousands. Dr.
Watson says thus: "I copy from the volume on my table
which I have just read with much gratification to myself,
and the highest respect for the author's science and
scholarship." After quoting Pliny, he says, "modern
wines with only their natural supply of alcohols are not
of strength equal to this. It is therefore reasonable to
infer that the art of distillation must have been known
to the vintners of antiquity. If so, it must have been
confined to some fraternity and practised by them as one
of their secret mysteries, for the purpose of fortifying
their wines, and thus kept secret until alcohol was discovered anew by the alchemists of the middle ages."
Such was Falernian, differing only from our Cognac

brandy from having a full vinous body with a luscious
fruity flavor.

This exposition of the true character of Falernian at
once explains and is confirmed by the fact that Horace
often in his exhortations to the hardest drinking, speaks
of some rules of mixing water with the Falernian, which
no Greek or Roman author mentions as usual as to other
wines, excepting only certain Greek wines of a similar
potency.

All the above stated considerations prove to my satisfaction (and I trust also to that of President King) that
Horace, with all his matchless merits, was exactly in the
state of certain of our mutual acquaintances, some of
whom, men of the prairie or of the plantation, alternate
between "total abstinence" and unquenchable thirst for
Bourbon and Monongahela; others, again, habitués of
city clubs and hotels, vibrate between soda or congress
water, and old Otard, or Geneva, more or less diluted
with water; generally less than more, and every day becoming more and more less.

Now to the inference from this statement of facts:
Would you, Mr. President, or you, Mr. Editor, take the
opinion or the evidence of any such, of our acquaintance,
though we should receive it with all respect on any other
point, political, commercial, or financial—upon any
question touching champagne. You would not? Neither
do I accept Horace's testimony on the same subject.

I learn that I have to meet another argument, levelled

at my Homeric interpretation, of the word commonly
rendered "dark," which I hold to mean "champagne-
faced," or covered with foam like champagne. This is
from another dignitary of learning, not of your city,
whose high scholarship is everywhere admitted. He is
armed with the authority and clothed with the dignity of
Jupiter, yet I cannot say with the Italian chief,

"Dii me terrent, et Jupiter hostis."

" The powers above I dread, and hostile Jove."

No, even against Jupiter, I reply,

" Thrice is he armed, who hath his quarrel just."

and I am thrice armed in the cause of truth and of
Homer.

As in respect to Horace, so in this Homeric question,
I defer for the present all mere verbal and lexicographical disquisition. My future readers will have quite
enough of it in my forthcoming volumes. But I willingly
meet the great argument of my very learned and eminent
critic, as it claims to rest upon broad, historical and
critical grounds.

He boldly maintains that Homer could not have known
personally anything of champagne—even supposing that
there was anything resembling it in his day—that
throughout his two epics he never intimates in himself or
in his heroes any taste or connoisseurship in wine, though
he describes the drinking of a good deal of it, to which
he gives various indiscriminating epithets, as "pleasant,"

"sweet," "divine," "dark," or "red." Above all, it is asserted that he betrays the grossest ignorance on its use in making his venerable Nestor (who should have known better) mix grated cheese with his old Pramnian wine.

Before entering on the wider field of discussion, I must briefly refute this last wholly unsound objection. It is easily and quickly done. Any reader who will carefully read the whole of the eleventh book of the Iliad, either in the original or in any tolerably faithful translation— even in Pope's brilliant but commonly loose paraphrase— will see at once that this preparation of old wine, thickened with grated goat's milk cheese, and flour, which Nestor took with his wounded friend after their escape from battle, was clearly a medical prescription prepared under the professional direction of Machaon, who was surgeon-general of the Greek allied army, as well as commanding colonel of his own and his brother's contingent. Machaon had a flesh wound ; Nestor, a very old man, was prostrated by fatigue and fright.

The word used is κυκεων, meaning a compound potion, and Pope with far more precision than is usual with him, renders it "the draught prescribed." I cannot help thinking that this happy version was suggested to the poet by his scholarly medical friend Dr. Arbuthnot, to whom he and Swift often expressed their warm acknowledgments for services, medical, literary and social :

> "——the kind Arbuthnot's aid,
> Who knows his art, but not his trade."

Dr. Holmes may very probably sneer at the prescribed
mixture, and I will not pretend to defend it, for that is
not in my line.   But Machaon was a physician of great
eminence in his day, and seems to have anticipated the
doctrines of Brown or of Broussais, and to have been
inclined to a bold practice in stimulants.   As a surgeon,
he stood at the very head of his profession.   Besides,
this was his prescription for himself, as well as for his
friend ; and when the physician thus shares with his patient the risk or the benefit of his potion, even Dr.
Holmes, heretic in medical faith as he is, will allow that
the patient may venture boldly to swallow whatever may
be ordered.   I trust that Dr. Watson will discuss this
whole question in the next edition of his *Medical Profession in Ancient Times.*   In the meanwhile, enough
has been said to exonerate both Homer and the Pylian
sage from the charge of heathenish ignorance in regard
to wine.

Indeed as to Nestor, even if the poet's frequent testi-
monials in the Iliad to his wisdom and vast knowledge
earned by old experience, are not enough to exempt him
from any suspicion of gross ignorance in respect to good
wine, he himself has given ample proof of his taste and
judgment in such matters in the Odyssey.   When the
son of Ulysses, in that epic, visits Nestor at his home in
Pylos, he finds the aged chief presiding at a grand sacrifice and banquet.   Before Nestor knows who his guest is
he greets him kindly, and besides ordering for him and

his friend a choice portion of the feast, gives them a goblet bumper of Malmsey Madeira.

Here I must pause and explain, to prevent the barking of small critics. Homer calls the wine μελιεύης—"honey-sweet"—which proves it to have been a luscious, sweet, fruity wine ; and all who are at all learned in the history of grape culture know that the Malmsey of Madeira is the product of a vine in Madeira, originally imported from the district of Malvasia, in the Peloponesus, which lay within Nestor's own territory. From Malvasia came the Spanish and Portuguese name of the wine, Malvasio ; thence the old French Malvoisie, and thence Malmsey. Pardon this apparent pedantry ; the digression is forced upon me. Nestor gives his unknown guests, with all the rest of the crowd, plenty of new, pleasant and sweet Malmsey of his own growth ; but afterward, when he knew that the son of his old friend was his guest, he gives him a more select entertainment with his family :

> ——" Filling high the cups
> With wine delicious, which the butler-dame
> Who kept his stores, in its eleventh year,
> Now first did broach."

In that compound of my own manufacture, "Butler-dame," I have aimed at clearly defining the office confided to confidential old ladies in well-regulated households in Greece, like Nestor's. Homer in his original Greek expresses the office, here and in seven or eight other places by the female substantive Ταμίη. The English and French translators all omit or slur it over, as if it was not genteel to have a female butler. The German translators, on the contrary, honestly use the resources of their noble language, as copious and flexible as the Greek, in its compounds, but give a rather broader sense, by *die haus-hof meisterin*. But I was not aware till after I had made my translation that the best Dutch translator, the illustrious Vondel, the Dryden of Holland, had formed a word of his own precisely parallel to my own, though more sonorous and musical, " *de schenckster-vrouw*. But I must restrain myself on these tempting verbal digressions (as I have done in my classical quotations), lest I should incur the Shakspearean sarcasm, he " has been at a great feast of languages and stolen the scraps." Let us return to Nestor.

Nestor never dreamed of giving his guests wine-whey, such as he had taken, according to prescription, nor does he offer them any grated cheese to mix with their new Malmsey, or their eleven years' old Pylian Particular.

Then, as to Homer's personal opportunities of becoming practically familiar with the good wines of his times, is it possible that my erudite critic imagines Homer to have led a straggling beggar-like life, like an Italian organ-grinder? The great bard has himself described his own *status* and habitual life in the picture he gives of the blind bard Domodoius, and the respect with which he is received, and the luxury he shares in at the sumptuous court of the good king Alconous. Like him, Ho-

mer himself passed from the table of one king, prince,
potentate or laird to that of another, faring sumptuously
every day, and thus becoming as familiar with the qualities
of the several Chian, Lesbian, Thrasian, Pramnain and
Pylian vintages, as our acquaintance Thackeray did with
the old Madeiras of Boston, Salem, Richmond and
Charleston, or the choice Bourdeaux and Rhine wines of
recherché tables in New York. I might quote an hundred
scattered lines in the Iliad to prove this. But why dwell
upon minor points of evidence? "The greatest is behind." While Homer ascribes this good taste and
knowledge of good wine to his wisest old man, has he
not distinguished that hero, who is second only in rank
to Achilles, by his taste and judgment in the same line?
Do not the plot and the interest of the second great epic
depend mainly upon this characteristic of its hero, and
the just pride he feels in his good cellar?

Alas! I ask these questions as if the answer was
familiar to all who read Homer even in the translations
of Pope or Cowper. Alas! alas! I do not know that a
single critic, or annotator, has explained—any Greek in-
structor or professor here or even in Germany has made
his students familiar with this great feature of Homer's
domestic epic, the Odyssey, and of its hero Ulysses.

Nevertheless, the filial piety of Virgil's Æneas—the
deep melancholy love of Tasso's Tancredi—the "noble
mind," "the courtier's, scholar's, soldier's eye, tongue,
sword," of the accomplished Hamlet are none of them

so essential a part of these several characters and of their eventful stories, as are to the character and story of Ulysses, his taste and skill in wine, his judgment and its management and use, and the deep interest which he manifests in his own fine and carefully selected stock.

In the very beginning of the Odyssey, before Ulysses himself appears on the scene, the poet, to make his reader acquainted with his hero's character, introduces him into the wine-room of the long-absent chief. It is quite worthy of remark that he is the only king or chief mentioned in either great epic, except Nestor, who had a regular, well-ordered wine-room, or cellar. These few chiefs, I must remind my readers, are repeatedly designated by the great poet, as the wisest of all the Greeks, so adjudged by the common voice—Nestor, from his varied experience and the collected wisdom he had gathered during the few generations of men among whom he had lived. Ulysses, from his own native sagacity. No other Greeks compared with them either in general wisdom, or in judgment in the choice or care of their wines.

Another proof of the true nature of this "wine," as Homer delicately calls it, is to be seen in the care with which the good priest kept it out of the way of all his servants, reserving it for the private drinking of himself and wife, of course in all moderation.

> " Of that pure drink, fit for the gods, no one
> Of all his household, male or female knew,
> Save only he, his wife and butler-dame."

By the way, this priest of Apollo seems to have been a sort of prince-bishop, keeping a large establishment of men and women servants. Yet he, too, like Newton and ·Ulysses, put his choice liquors and stores under the care of a butleress, or, as I have preferred to render it in a more Homeric phrase, and in the spirit of the Greek compound, a Butler-dame.

Achilles, for instance, was a model of gentlemanly hospitality, carved beautifully, and gave his guests the best wine that force or money could get: but he had no stock of it, and did not know how to manage it, if he had it. Not so the "much-contriving" Ulysses.

Before Ulysses enters upon the scene, his son, Telemachus is described as preparing for a secret voyage in search of his long-absent father, and this affords Homer an opportunity to paint in anticipation, though indirectly, the most striking peculiarities of his hero. His cellar, or wine-room (for it appears to have been above ground, though on the ground-floor), is superintended, like that of Nestor, by an aged female butler. I am not quite satisfied with any translator, and I render the lines thus:

> " Down to a broad, high room, the youth descends,
> His father's store-room, where his treasures lay :
> There stood against the wall, in order ranged,
> Casks of age-ripened wine, fit for the gods,
> The grape's pure juice, from every mixture free."

The good young man, who had been well brought up

14

by his mother, according to his father's precepts and example, thus gave order touching the providing for his ship:

> " Fill up these demijohns ; draw off bright wine—
> Our best, next after that thou dost reserve
> Hapless Ulysses, still expecting home ;
> If, death escaping, he shall e'er return,
> Fill twelve, then fit them all with stoppers tight."

I translate as literally as metre will permit, in honest, "English verse, without rhyme" (as Milton phrases it), in the hope of preserving these minutely graphic touches of the great poet, who always narrates to the eye, and in turn displays " *la terribil via*," the grand and terrible manner of Michael Angelo, or the grace, dignity and expression of Raphael, and then rivals the most painstaking Dutch or Flemish painter in his careful details of the butchery, the barn-yard, the market, the kitchen or the wine cellar.

I flatter myself that in spite of the obvious difficulty of such passages, I have, in the above and my other scraps of Homeric versions, succeeded in expressing some exquisite details which Pope's rhymes have polished into vague smoothness, and Cowper's more faithful, but too uniformly Miltonic, blank verse has failed to render.

After this preliminary sketch of the "many planning" Ulysses, we find him everywhere taking his wine like a gentleman, never in any excess, but always with good taste, whether at the table of the magnificent king of

Pharacia or at the humble fireside of the keeper of his own hogs. He avoids the snares of Circe by refusing to drink her brewed and drugged liquor. When he explored the land of the Cyclops, he took with him a goat-skin of high proof brandy, given him by the priest of Apollo, which he used only in case of accidents. I say "BRANDY;" for though Homer calls it wine, that must have been from delicacy toward the reverend gentleman, for the poet expressly says that the worthy priest and his wife were wont:

> Whene'er they quaffed that dark, delicious juice,
> To slake each cup with twenty from the fount,
> Yet the slaked bowl sweet odor shed around,
> Divine, enticing.

But Ulysses took none of this brandy himself, nor gave it to his men, but when he got into a scrape with the giant Cyclops, he dosed the huge cannibal with it quite raw, which soon made him tipsy (or, as the original expresses it with philosophical accuracy "came around his brain,") then puts him to sleep, when Ulysses puts out his great single eye, and escapes.

When he reaches home *incog.*, he learns with indignation the suit of the petty chiefs of Ithaca to his supposed widow, their wasteful depredations upon his goods and chattels, especially his cattle and hogs, and their insults to his only son; but he does not explode in full wrath till he hears of the wasteful abuse of his wines—the οἶνον

διαφυσσόμενον (as he says with the precision of a carefulwine
merchant), his good wine " drawn off." This he de-
nounces as the " unkindest cut of all." He successively
recounts his wrongs from the suitors of his wife :

> " Their shameless acts, guests roughly drawn away,
> Through all the house gross insults to the maids,
> Provision gormandized day after day :
> The wine drawn off, drunk up with monstrous waste,
> Enormous, without stint, or taste, or end."
>
> Od. XVi.

I have not time nor space to note his other expressions
of wrath on the same topic.

It is, therefore, with admirable fitness that the poet
makes Ulysses defer the hour of his final vengeance till
he sees his palace filled with revelry, and the wine cup
crowned with his own best vintages, lifted high and passed
around by the insolent invaders of his home and his
honor. Then it is, when the loudest and boldest of these
revellers lifts to his head a huge two-handled goblet of
choice Ithaca Reserve, that he who had long watched
these scenes in suppressed wrath, and in the guise and
garb of a beggar, now "throws off his patience and
his rags together," rises from the mendicant into the
monarch, and from his mighty bow showers around winged
arrowy vengeance upon the wretches who had essayed to
win the affections of his wife, who had plundered his
possessions, who had wronged and insulted his darling
only son, and who had swilled, without appreciating it,

pipe after pipe of his much prized wine, all of it carefully selected, in splendid condition, and most of it more than twenty years old.

And this is the Homer who had no taste, judgment, feeling, or knowledge in wine!

But I have said more than enough on these topics. Those who wish to know still more on them must be content to wait until the publication of my "Lectures on Homeric Literature," unless, indeed, I should find time to comply with the urgent solicitations of your great publishers—the Appletons—and supply the article Ulysses for the American Cyclopædia. I have done with all journalistic controversy. I have floored my adversaries, and may now say like Virgil's veteran pugilist :

> "Hic victor cestus artemque, repono ;"

or, as I have rendered the line in my yet unpublished translation of Virgil :

> "Still Victor, Champion, now with pride
> My *science* and my gloves I lay aside."

Very truly your friend,